BY JOHNNY MARCIANO
AND EMILY CHENOWETH

KLAWDE

EVIL ALIEN WARLORD CAT

ILLUSTRATED BY
ROBB
MOMMAERTS

PENGUIN WORKSHOP

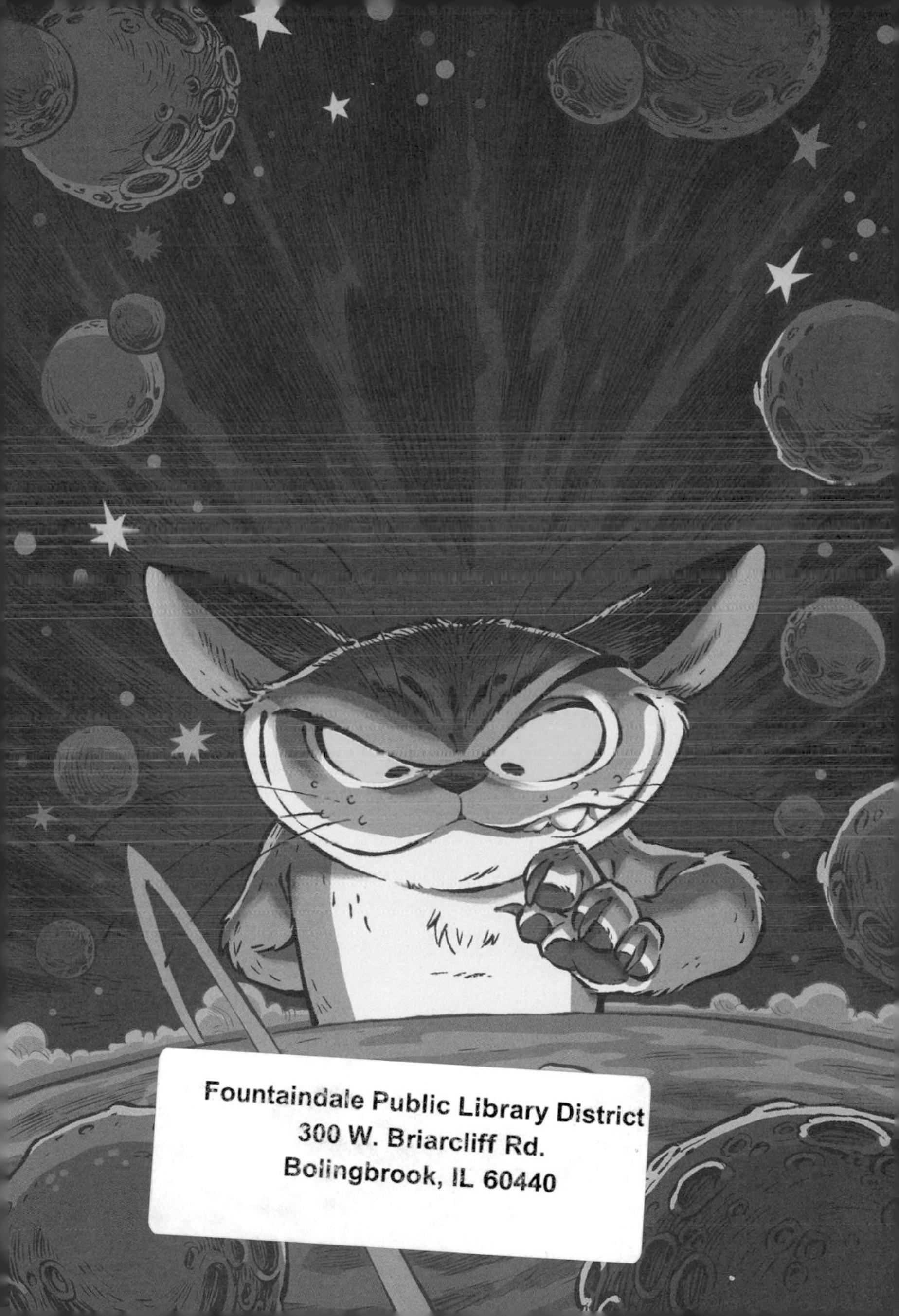

For Raja and Rajeev, who made
high school less worse than it was—JM

For Eliza and Josephine,
who really, *really* love cats—EC

For Allie, Nick, and Maureen, who make
my life a very happy one—RM

W

PENGUIN WORKSHOP
An Imprint of Penguin Random House LLC, New York

Text copyright © 2019 by John Bemelmans Marciano and Emily Chenoweth. Illustrations copyright © 2019 by Robb Mommaerts. All rights reserved. Published by Penguin Workshop, an imprint of Penguin Random House LLC, New York. PENGUIN and PENGUIN WORKSHOP are trademarks of Penguin Books Ltd, and the W colophon is a registered trademark of Penguin Random House LLC. Manufactured in China.

Visit us online at www.penguinrandomhouse.com.

Library of Congress Control Number: 2018061170

ISBN 9781524787202   10 9 8 7

PROLOGUE

DATE: THE 789TH DAY

OF THE YEAR 58-493-D

PLANET: LYTTYRBOKS

PLACE: THE SUPREMEST COURT

OF ALL GALACTIC ORDER

My enemies came for me at naptime.

Before I could even unsheathe my claws, they

pounced atop me. They tied me up and chained my

paws, and then they dragged me from my holding cell

into the Supremest Court of All Galactic Order.

It was a most unpleasant way to wake up.

Though I could not fight them, I yowled so

ferociously that the courtroom crowd—**traitors**, all of them!—hissed and scattered.

Only *one* cat had not betrayed me: my loyal minion, Flooffee-Fyr.

"You'll always be *my* Lord High Emperor!" he called. "And I will always be your—*oww*!"

Someone had smacked him on the back of the head. It was the greatest traitor of them all, my former second-in-command—General Ffangg!

"Not such a mighty and powerful warlord *now*, are you?" he said, purring.

My tail slashed in anger. "I shall have my REVENGE on you, Ffangg!"

"We shall see about that," Ffangg said, and bared his teeth at me as the Thirteen Noble Elders filed into the room.

The Chief Elder licked his right paw and called the court to order.

"My fellow cats," he began. "Thousands of years ago, when our planet was overrun by criminal felines, our wise ancestors decided that these evildoers must be exiled.

"Far across the universe, they discovered a vast wasteland of a planet, inhabited by a race of carnivorous ogres. For generations, we sent our convicts there. None ever returned. But in the year 49-763-B, the punishment was deemed *too* cruel, and it was decreed that no feline—no matter how evil, no matter how tyrannical—would ever again be sent to this horrible place. And so it has been.

"Until **you** came along.

"You, former Lord High Emperor, have been so relentless in clawing your way to power, so ruthless in your evil schemes of domination, and so dedicated to general crimes against felinity, that we are forced to resurrect this ancient punishment."

The crowd gasped.

"Have you anything to say, Wyss-Kuzz?" asked the Chief Elder.

A lesser cat might have begged for mercy, but all I showed them was my scorn! "Every one of you feckless felines will rue the day you overthrew me—the greatest warlord the universe has ever known—for the likes of a pathetic schemer like General Ffangg! You may shoot me into space like yesterday's trash, but I swear to you that one day soon, I WILL BE BACK!"

General Ffangg chuckled. "*You* will be an ogre's breakfast."

With a wave of Ffangg's paw, the guards unbound me and forced me into the waiting teleporter. Brilliant green light flashed as the wormhole opened. In an instant, I was transported 2,900.4 million light-years across space—to the most horrible, distant, and desolate planet in the universe:

Earth.

CHAPTER 1

Saturday.

It was a rainy Saturday night, and I was lying on the floor of my new living room, staring at the ceiling and wishing I were anywhere but here. Dad was watching baseball, Mom was working on her laptop, and I was experiencing a life-threatening level of boredom.

I still couldn't believe what had happened. Up until last week, I'd been living a really great life in Brooklyn, New York. But then my parents decided to move 2,900.4 miles across the country to here.

Elba, Oregon.

If you ask me—and no one did—this was a terrible idea.

In New York, I could visit three friends without ever leaving my apartment building. And when I did leave,

I could walk to the library, a comic book store, a candy shop, and two pizzerias all without having to cross the street.

If I left my house in Elba, I could walk to twelve trees, an ant mound, a hornets' nest, and a bunch of rosebushes. Nature was *everywhere*.

It was spooky.

According to my mom, we'd moved to Oregon because she'd gotten a better job, and I got to have a big bedroom and a backyard.

But that stuff didn't matter to me. Where were the comic book stores and pizza places? There wasn't a single shop on my street—not even a laundromat with good vending machines!

Here in Oregon, I had nothing to do and zero friends. Which was maybe why I hadn't unpacked yet.

But then again, neither had my parents. What *their* excuse was, I had no idea.

I'd just picked up the latest Americaman comic to read for the millionth time when *it* happened—a bright green flash lighting up the sky outside the window. It only lasted a second, and then everything went dark and rainy again.

"Did you see that?" I asked.

"Yes!" my dad hollered. "Torres stole third base! *Third base!*"

"No, that crazy green light!"

My mom looked up from her laptop. "What, dear?"

"The *green* light outside!" I said.

"Oh, Raj, that was just lightning," my mom said.

Okay, so another weird thing about Oregon: *green lightning*.

I went back to reading my comic—and then the doorbell rang.

DING-DONG!

The doorbell? Who could *that* be?

CHAPTER 2

Here I was.

Alone.

On *Earth*.

It was even more horrifying than the ancient texts had described.

It was nighttime. Blazing lights shone down from the top of huge, branchless trees. As I scanned the area for carnivorous ogres and other dangers, something *wet* hit me on the nose.

There was a liquid, falling from the sky!

Was this some sort of chemical weapon? Was I under attack?

I rushed under a leafy bush, but it offered little protection. The liquid slid down my lustrous fur, chilling me to the bone. I didn't know *what* it could possibly be, but I HATED it. I had to find shelter now!

Thankfully, many of the trees on this planet did have branches. I climbed the nearest one, from which I immediately found evidence of Humans.

All around stood their massive fortresses, packed in so close they almost touched one another. High wooden walls surrounded their small patches of territory. In front of the fortresses sat huge, tank-like vehicles.

This must be a very warlike planet indeed.

I needed to gain entry into one of these fortified structures. I didn't know what the ogres within would do to me, but this falling liquid was *intolerable*.

I raced to the nearest fortress. Next to its front portal was a glowing button. A push-button to open the entrance! Perhaps this would allow me to sneak in without being noticed. I leaped up and pressed it.

DING-DONG!

Hiss! Why did it make that awful *noise*?

CHAPTER 3

Still Saturday.

"Did anyone else hear that?" I asked.

"Hear what?" my mom said. When she was working, the world could end and she wouldn't notice.

"The doorbell!"

"It must have been the TV, dear," Mom said, still not looking up from her laptop. "We don't have friends here yet."

That was for sure.

DING-DONG!

There it went again! I got up and peeked through the front-door window, but I couldn't see anyone.

Then I heard a horrible noise. It sounded like a possum being electrocuted.

Was it some kind of *nature*? Right at our front door?

Back home, the closest I ever got to nature was when I watched pigeons fighting over pizza crusts on the sidewalk.

Living here was **terrifying**.

Finally, the awful squealing stopped. Nervously, I opened the door and peered into the darkness.

There was a *cat* sitting on our welcome mat.

That terrible sound had been meowing!

"Was that you?" I said. "What are you doing here, kitty?" And then I felt really stupid, because cats can't talk.

The cat was skinny, wet from the rain, and didn't have a collar.

Maybe he was a stray. Maybe I could *keep* him. I had always wanted a pet—*especially* a cat—and now one had appeared on my doorstep!

I was about to try to pet him when he raced between my legs into the house.

"AHHHH!" My mom shrieked like she'd seen a rat.

I ran into the living room. Mom was clutching her chest and staring at the cat, who was frozen in a low crouch.

"Where did that *thing* come from?" she said. "And why is it in our house?"

"He was on the porch," I said. "The doorbell rang, and there he was!"

My dad smiled. "Maybe it's a welcome-to-the-neighborhood gift!"

My mother did not smile. "A plate of cookies is a welcome-to-the-neighborhood gift. A *cat* is a reason to call animal control."

"Can we keep him?" I asked.

Mom looked at me like I was insane.

"Here, kitty kitty kitty," Dad said, reaching out a hand to pet him. The cat swatted at him with his paw.

"It's probably feral," Mom said.

"No, he's not!" I said, even though I had no idea what *feral* meant. "He's just scared. Can I keep him? *Please?*"

My parents looked at each other, then at me. Then we all turned to the cat. He was staring right back at us.

He meowed.

At least, I *think* that's what that sound was.

CHAPTER 4

Though I feared the button's infernal noise would summon the Humans, I jumped up and struck it a second time.

DING-DONG!

Still the portal remained shut. I attempted to get a better look at the glowing button. Maybe it was operated by paw-print recognition technology. Were these Humans less primitive than was believed?

Perhaps I could *ask* them for help.

It was a dangerous idea. According to the ancient histories, Humans were ugly, brutal, and stupid. But right now they were my only hope.

"Humans, hear me!" I cried. "I am a poor and hungry traveler from a distant planet!"

Still nothing.

I was about to seek shelter in a different fortress when the portal slowly opened. Out peered a creature more hideous than my worst nightmare.

The monster was as big as twenty cats, and it stood on two legs.

But the most shocking, *dreadful* thing was that this beast

HAD

NO

FUR!!!

I froze—which was worse? This monster, or the falling liquid?

I raced between the Human's legs.

Inside was dry, but there were two **more** Humans, and these were even bigger and *more* hideous!

I sank into Defensive Crouch. The largest ogre reached toward me, and I batted its monstrous, hairless paw aside. But there was no way I could overwhelm them all! They were too gigantic!

My only defense, I realized, was disguise.

"Please, do me no harm," I said as sweetly as possible. "I am just a lost and innocent astronaut."

I don't think the Humans understood my sophisticated language.

Their own speech was as ugly as their long, whiskerless faces. What came out of their mouths was an incomprehensible mix of slurring and grunting.

I could understand that they were arguing over me,

however. The small ogre sought to offer me protection, but the big ones were not convinced.

Little could these humongous hairless Humans know that standing before them was the **GREATEST FELINE WARLORD** the universe had ever known.

CHAPTER 5

Saturday Continued.

"Is that thing meowing?" Mom asked. "It sounds like a wolverine being burned alive."

"I think this little fella must be part Siamese!" Dad said.

"I don't care what kind of breed the cat is," I said. "I want him."

I promised my parents that I'd pay for his cat food out of my allowance—that I'd do his litter box—that I'd even clean my room AND make my bed every day.

My dad shrugged and went back to watching baseball, knowing the decision wasn't up to him. Meanwhile, my mom eyed the cat suspiciously as he leaped up to the windowsill.

He gazed down at us like a furry gargoyle.

"Are we sure it even *is* a cat?" Mom said. "It's awfully strange-looking."

"Don't insult him," I said.

"Its brain is the size of a walnut," my mom said. "It doesn't know if I'm insulting it or praising its beauty."

"Can I keep him? Please?"

Mom sighed. "All right," she said.

I couldn't believe it! It was a miracle—I was going to get what I wanted! That *never* happened.

"Thank you, thank you, thank you," I said. "You've made the right decision, I swear."

She nodded, and then she held out a brochure. "On *one* condition," she said.

I should've known there'd be a condition.

"You keep the cat, you go to nature camp," she said. "It starts Monday."

Nature. And *camp.*

Two words that struck terror into my heart.

YOU'LL GO WILD FOR NATURE at

CAMP ECLIPSE!

Discover the SKILLS OF SURVIVAL on the slopes of an EXTINCT VOLCANO!

Together with your **FOREST PACK**, you will learn how to:

- ☑ Build a **SHELTER** out of branches and leaves!
- ☑ Identify the tracks of **WILD ANIMALS!**
- ☑ Understand the **LANGUAGE** of birds!
- ☑ **FORAGE** the **WILDERNESS** for **FOOD!**
- ☑ **CLIMB** trees!
- ☑ Test the limits of your **MENTAL** and **PHYSICAL ENDURANCE!**
- ☑ And BEST OF ALL, play the life-changing **GAME** of **SURVIVAL NIGHT!!!!**

"Is all this going to happen *outside*?" I asked.

"I should certainly think so," Mom said.

I really didn't want to go. But I also really wanted the cat.

I gulped and nodded.

"Fine," I said. "I'll do it."

The cat blinked and swished his tail. He was so adorable and innocent, I'd do *anything* to keep him.

CHAPTER 6

The smallest ogre now appeared to be begging the long-furred ogre for some kind of mercy. I sensed that the long-furred one was the warlord of the fortress, while the small one was some kind of underling. The largest, baldest ogre was clearly lowly as well.

I observed the Humans as they communicated in their barbaric tongue. They *did* have some fur, but it sprouted from their bodies in strange places, such as the tops of their heads and in lines above their eyes. Bizarre!

Unsurprisingly, they were so disgusted by their own appearance that they had draped themselves in a kind of fur-substitute, held together with primitive buttons and zippers.

I almost felt sorry for them.

All of a sudden, the small ogre scooped me up in its

arms and hurried down a passageway to its lair.

"Put me down!" I commanded.

But it did not obey. It held me so tightly I couldn't get away. I watched in horror as its huge mouth came right at my head.

It was going to EAT me!

With all my strength, I tried to push the monster away, but I could not overpower it.

The Human put its lips to my fur and made a loud smacking sound. And then—*it let me go*.

What did this *mean*? Before I could even begin to ponder it, something even stranger happened: The ogre stretched out on a soft platform, covered itself with a large piece of cloth, and *died*.

I pawed its chest cautiously, fearing this was some kind of trick. But there was no getting it back to life. In the next room, I found the other two Humans had perished similarly.

Had their enemies poisoned them?

I could hardly believe my luck! Now I had a large, well-equipped fortress all to myself. Once I located the Humans' weapons and teleporter, I could make my way back to Lyttyrboks and reclaim what was rightfully mine.

Purrr.

First, however, I had to do something about the pitiful state of my fur. The foul falling liquid had made it damp and clumpy.

But what could I do? Without a follicular exuviator, I would have to . . . to . . . *lick* myself! Like some sort of barbarian tree cat!

It took all night. I was finally finishing when Earth's puny, pale sun rose into the sky, and the strangest, most disturbing thing yet occurred.

The Humans began to ARISE.

They lumbered about with half-opened eyes.

ZOMBIES! They were **GIANT OGRE ZOMBIES!!**

I went to the front portal, but I couldn't open it!

I was **trapped**!

As I madly searched for an escape route, the Humans one by one went into a small room where they removed their primitive coverings and stepped into a tall glass cage. Then they turned a knob, which caused that horrible clear liquid to come streaming down over their hideous bodies.

Moments later, they came out, wearing new coverings and *smiling*.

What kind of world *was* this?

CHAPTER 7

Sunday Morning.

I woke up happier than I'd been in weeks. I had my own cat! I'd been asking for one ever since I was six, and it had *finally* happened.

After breakfast, my mom said we needed to start unpacking, but my dad insisted we go out for cat supplies.

"But almost everything we own is still in boxes!" Mom said.

"Well, I unpacked my signed Derek Jeter baseball," Dad said, pointing to where it sat on the mantel. "And that's all *I* need to feel at home!"

Mom sighed. "Fine," she said. "You two go to PetBin. They do free vaccinations on weekends. Make sure that thing gets a rabies shot."

"You bet!" Dad said brightly.

Getting my new cat into the carrier that my dad had borrowed was no picnic. It took both of us, and my dad got so scratched up that it looked like he might need medical attention.

I tried to think of names for the cat while we drove, but it was hard to concentrate because Dad was blasting his eighties hair metal music.

We're not gonna take it!

NO! We ain't gonna take it!

We're not gonna take it ANYMOOOOORE!

I really, really wished he wouldn't sing along.

At PetBin, Dad filled the cart with supplies. My cat—Bandit? Or Hermes? No, *Loki*!—seemed a little more relaxed now. He was purring.

Or was he growling? It was hard to tell.

The last thing we picked up was a collar with a name tag.

"What would you like me to put on it?" the cashier asked when we went to get it engraved.

I was still thinking Loki—or maybe Thor?—when my dad blurted out something that sounded like "Claude."

"Clod?" the cashier said

"No," Dad said. "*Klawde*. K L A W-D-E, like *clawed*, but spelled in a more exciting way!" He playfully pawed at the air. "Why use a *C* when you could use a *K*? *K* is the alphabet's party letter!"

Dad looked so pleased with himself that I didn't have the heart to protest. I told myself that I had my cat, and that was all that really mattered.

While the cashier was engraving the tag, we took Klawde over to where they were offering the free vaccinations.

A young-looking vet opened the carrier door and bent down to see inside. Klawde's purr-growl stopped.

"Oh, look at him, he's so . . ." The vet paused. "*Interesting*-looking."

Klawde was crouched down low and baring his fangs.

"Maybe we shouldn't give him a shot right now," I said.

"Oh no, it's fine!" the vet said. "I work with animals every day, and I know how to handle them."

He reached into the cage and pulled Klawde out by the scruff of the neck.

"See?" he said. "Easy peasy! Now we just take this needle and—"

With a bloodcurdling yowl, Klawde flew at the vet's face and *latched on.*

The vet started screaming and flailing his arms around. I was yelling, "STOP! STOP!" and my dad was desperately trying to pull Klawde off.

It wasn't so easy peasy after all.

CHAPTER 8

Just when I thought I was safe, the Humans brought out the cage.

I struggled valiantly, but together the two ogres overpowered me. After locking me inside, the small ogre carried me into their armored vehicle and we proceeded to leave the fortress.

Had my enemies somehow made contact with them?

Is my exile not enough for you, General Ffangg? Do you now intend to kill me?!

At the end of a seemingly endless journey, they removed my cage from the vehicle. The landscape was the most awful and desolate I had ever seen.

The building they took me into was some kind of prison. And inside were more cages—filled with other cats!

The legends were true! Lyttyrboks's criminal felines had survived their exile—and their descendants were right *here*!

I tried calling to them. "Fellow cats! Comrades! What sort of evil place is this?"

But the only word I heard back from them was "MROW!"

MROW? Did Earth cats have their own language? What could this word mean? *Beware? Turn back?*

Before I could make sense of it, the ogres began to wheel me around the room in a small vehicle made of metal bars. They filled this vehicle with many boxes and bags. It was hard to see out of the cage, but there appeared to be pictures of cats on the boxes.

I could not understand what was happening.

The next thing I knew, my cage was being lifted up. The door opened, and I shrank back. I would not let them leave me in this horrible place! But then a new

Human reached inside the cage and grabbed me by the neck. He was lightning fast! Suddenly I was out in the open—exposed!—and being held down by its hideous five-fingered paw. Then it drew out a tiny spear and tried to stab me in the neck!

I attacked!

First, my claws ripped at its hands. Next, its face.

Oh, how sweet the feeling! I left long red scratch marks all over its vile, furless cheeks. When I was but seconds away from murdering it, my Humans pulled me off.

This was followed by much incomprehensible yelling as the bleeding Human chased my Humans out of its territory.

CHAPTER 9

Sunday Afternoon.

My dad didn't play any eighties music on the ride home from PetBin. He looked sort of grim.

I kept sneaking glances at Klawde, safely back in his cat carrier. When dogs do something bad, they look guilty. Not Klawde.

He was *definitely* purring now.

Dad cleared his throat. "What happened at PetBin—"

"You're not going to make me give him away, are you?" I said. "Because I don't have any friends here, and if I don't get to keep Klawde, I'll be all alone and miserable!"

"Raj," he said, "you *are* going to make friends. At Camp Eclipse."

"Don't remind me," I said.

"But what I was *going* to say is that the vet took a gamble with Klawde today, and he lost. You did warn him."

"So I can keep Klawde?"

My dad nodded. "But you and he had better be careful. If that animal scratches your mother—"

"It'll be the last thing he ever does," I said.

"Exactly."

I peered into Klawde's cage. "Did you hear that, boy? You've got to be *nice*."

Klawde looked me right in the eyes and blinked. He almost seemed to understand what I was saying.

And then he hacked up a giant hairball.

CHAPTER 10

Oh, the humiliations of exile! A hairball! I *had* to
find an exuviating robot on this planet.

Back at the fortress, the Humans released me from
the cage and opened the items they had stolen from the
Territory of the Bleeding Man. And then they placed
them before me . . . like an *offering*.

Did they realize I was their superior? Were they
pledging their undying loyalty to me? This would be
most excellent.

I inspected their gifts.

There was a small tower with rope wound around it.
A sculpture, maybe?

There were also several fluffy, fake animals that
they tried to coax me into attacking and killing. Was this
their idea of military training?

These were disappointing offerings indeed.

They next took out a box, poured some sort of sand into it, and attached a cover. They kept lifting me up and placing me inside. I had no idea what they wanted me to do in there. Dig? But why?

Finally, there was the food—if you could even call it that. The only reason I knew they expected me to eat the pebble-like pellets was the way the big ogre kept pretending to put them into its mouth.

Not that *he* was eating the pellets. No, the Humans had something altogether different to dine on.

Strange smells—delicious smells—came from a pot that the long-furred Human was stirring. I spit out the pellets and jumped near the flaming metal box to sample this food, but the long-furred Human pushed me off.

The *gall*! If only I had my molecular disintegrator, I would have vaporized it. Did this ogre have any *idea* what I did to the entire population of Poosikat?

I again leaped to the firebox, and again was shoved off.

We shall *see* about this.

CHAPTER 11

Monday Morning.

Mount Eclipse Welcome Cabin *500 Feet*—the sign read.

Even though we'd pulled into the parking lot, I was still desperately trying to get out of the whole nature camp thing.

Mom refused to listen. "Look, Raj," she said as we walked away from the car. "This camp is a wonderful opportunity for you to understand the natural world, learn important survival skills, and beef up your college applications."

"But I'm going into *sixth* grade!" I said. "And I thought the point of camp was to make friends."

"Oh, yes, of course. Friends." Mom pointed at a

group of kids who looked two years older than me. "How about *them*?" she said.

As Mom signed me in to camp, I watched the kids stab at trees with pocketknives. I had no idea what they were doing, but they did *not* look friendly.

When I turned back, my mom was already walking to our Prius. "Have fun!" she called, and drove away.

Fun. Yeah, right.

"Hi! What's your forest name?"

A girl had just *materialized* in front of me, like some kind of nature ninja. Her face was painted with mud.

"My *what*?"

The dried mud was cracking on her cheeks. It looked itchy.

"At Camp Eclipse, everyone has a forest name. Mine is Cedar," she said.

Before I could say anything, I felt a big hand press down on my shoulder. I turned around to see a kid the size of a refrigerator looming over me.

"I'm Wolf," he said.

"That's a great forest name!" Cedar said.

"That's my *real* name," the big guy said. "My forest name is Steve."

Cedar and I looked at each other. It seemed like a bad idea to correct him.

"What's *your* name?" Steve asked me.

"I'm Raaaaa . . ." I started to say *my* real name, but *that* was wrong, so I thought fast and finished, ". . . aaat."

Rat? Did I just name myself Rat? Did they even *have* rats in nature?

Steve grinned. "That's cool."

"We're going to learn so much in nature camp! You guys are going to love it!" Cedar cried. "I can't wait until Survival Night!"

Just as I was about to ask what Survival Night meant exactly, the sound of a strange hissing animal filled the air.

Except it wasn't an animal. It was a tall, skinny guy with a big, bushy beard. He was standing on top of a large stump and flapping his long arms.

Cedar told us that this was the park ranger, who was also our camp counselor. "*His* forest name is Turkey Vulture."

"Why is he hissing?" I asked. "Is there something wrong with him?"

"No. It's the sound of a turkey vulture, duh! That's how he calls us to the Speaking Stump," Cedar said. "Follow me."

I looked at the counselor again. I didn't care what Cedar said—there was *definitely* something wrong with him.

CHAPTER 12

With the Humans gone, I had the fortress to myself. It was time to locate their intergalactic teleporter and return to my planet to have my **revenge**!

Finding it proved difficult, however.

For one thing, the Humans put portals *between* their rooms for some reason. And like everything else on this barbaric planet, they were designed for opposable thumbs.

Hiss! Why couldn't they just use universal touch screens for everything like we did back home?

I took a nap and considered what to do.

Five minutes later, I was hungry.

The food situation had thus far been intolerable. Worse even than the petrified pellets was the foul-smelling canned sludge they seemed to think was a treat for me.

Their food they placed inside an enormous box that was divided into two compartments. Using all my strength, I managed to pull one compartment open.

The food inside was frozen solid. But *why*?

The second compartment, however, held items that were merely cold.

I licked everything.

Much of what the Humans considered food disgusted me. There was, however, a long yellow rectangle that was rather tasty, and an even more delicious white liquid inside a carton.

I also found a box of twelve smooth brown ovals. I bit into one. It cracked open, and a yellow-orange glob suspended in a thick clear goo oozed out.

I ate it.

It was **DISGUSTING**!

I went and vomited into one of the ogres' foot coverings.

CHAPTER 13

Monday Morning.

The park ranger kept hissing and flapping until we'd all gathered around the big stump he was standing on.

Then he smiled at us. Was it just me, or did he have a *lot* of teeth?

"Welcome to Camp Eclipse, nature newbies. My name is Turkey Vulture, and I am your Survival Leader.

Before we begin today's activities, let us put on our deer ears!"

I looked over at Cedar and the older kids, who were all cupping their hands behind their ears. I did the same, and the sounds around me—birds, wind, insects—got louder.

"This is the sound of . . . *nature*!" Turkey Vulture said.

It sounded pretty nice, actually. Not nearly as spooky as I'd expected.

"Some fear that humans are destroying the planet, but Earth will be here long after we are gone. Nature is indestructible," Turkey Vulture went on. "Humans, on the other hand, are not."

He paused dramatically.

"However, if you learn to live *with* nature, there is hope for you. When you begin to understand nature's secrets, you may be able to survive the future that is coming. The day when you can no longer just buy whatever you want, such as soda, skateboards, pants"—and here he looked straight at me—"or Americaman comic books, in a *store*."

I felt a chill up my spine. It was like he could see right into my soul!

Then he smiled with all those teeth again. "The first step is to learn to navigate our way in nature," Turkey Vulture went on. "Does anyone have an idea how we do this?"

It seemed like everyone *except* me was raising their hands, but Turkey Vulture called on me anyway.

I gulped. "Well, once my dad and I got off the highway at a rest stop that was *really* nature-y behind the parking lot. We went for a walk and got super lost, but we used Google Earth to find our way to an In-N-Out Burger."

Everyone just stared at me.

"Uh, and then we called a car, which took us back

to the . . . um . . . rest stop."

The other kids began to snicker and looked to see what Turkey Vulture would say.

The camp counselor narrowed his eyes at me. "Do you have a phone on you *now*?" he asked.

I said yes.

He shuddered in horror.

"Does anyone *else* have any technology?"

Steve raised his hand. "Does an iPad count?"

One of the older kids—who I'd heard called Scorpion—said, "What a bunch of *losers* these little kids are!"

After walking Steve and me to the cabin with the WELCOME sign on it, Turkey Vulture made us put our devices into what he called the Forbidden Basket. Then he led all of us under the giant Camp Eclipse arch, which he said represented the gateway between civilization and nature.

As I walked through, Turkey Vulture wrinkled his nose. "The stench of civilization is strong on you, camper."

It wasn't meant as a compliment, but I took it as one.

CHAPTER 14

I took a nap and then resumed my search for a teleporter.

There were large brown boxes scattered throughout the fortress, and I had discovered that this was where the Humans kept their technology. If you could even call it that. It was all so primitive. And nothing even worked!

Enraged, I batted at the thin black tail of the nearest appliance. Almost all their technological objects had tails with three silver prongs at the tip. Were they for decoration?

Everything *does* look better with a tail, after all.

Then I noticed several holes in the wall that were the same size as the silver prongs on the tails. Perhaps this was a power source?

I inserted the prongs into the wall, and the object
sent hot air **blasting** into my face!

HISS!

I shut it off and began putting more tail prongs into wall holes.

The results were extremely disappointing. Most of the Humans' apparatuses had to do with creating light or heat. After more searching, I found what I hoped was a photon gun, but the wire contraptions at the end of it did not fire ten gigajoules of electricity. They just spun around.

I could not imagine what this was for. You could barely maim even one enemy at a time with it!

On the bright side, the brown boxes were satisfying in their own right. Like our wonderful sleeping quarters back home. I got in one and took a nap.

Refreshed, I looked through more of the boxes, but it was hopeless. These ogres did not *have* multiphasic glob coils or photonic scramblers, let alone an intergalactic teleporter.

I would have to build one myself out of their junk. It could take weeks! And where would I even work?

The only place I had any privacy was in the covered box filled with sand.

I brought their most promising piece of technology inside the box and began to take it apart. It had a timing mechanism and a spinning tray, and it created radiation. Useful.

I had finally realized what they wanted me to do in that covered box, by the way.

Pee. And *poop*.

The Humans apparently wanted to *collect* feline excrement. Why, I had no idea, but I refused to supply them with it. Instead, I relieved myself where they did: in a room that contained a shiny white bowl half-filled with a small pool of liquid.

With one press of a lever, the pee and poop were flushed away and *voilà*! A fresh pool appeared.

It was certainly their most interesting device.

Where *were* those terrible Humans, anyway? They had been gone many naptimes. Would they ever return?

I feared the battle had gone poorly for them.

CHAPTER 15

Monday Evening.

"So, did you have fun at nature camp?" my mom asked when she got home.

"It's *survival* camp," I said. "Did you even read about this place before you signed me up?"

"Of course I did! Your new school recommended it."

"Well, it was *not* fun. We played Hide-or-Get-Eaten."

"That sounds amusing," she said.

"It was terrifying!"

And it *was*. We got split into two groups: predators and prey. Cedar told me it was just nature tag, but Scorpion and his pals took the kill-or-get-killed concept way too seriously. Their idea of tag was to shove the younger kids into the mud and try to step on us.

"I see you did some arts and crafts, too." Mom held up my name badge, which was a cross section of a tree on a necklace of twine. "R-A-T. Why does it say *Rat*?"

"It's my forest name, Mom. And it's written in blood. *My* blood."

"You have such an imagination, Raj!"

It was actually just beet juice, but it might as well have been blood.

"You *really* need to work on your handwriting, however," she said.

Before she could assign me penmanship drills, I went to find Klawde. Instead I found Dad, wandering around the kitchen looking confused.

"Have you seen my flashlight?" he asked. "Or the microwave?"

"Sorry."

He poked his head into one of the moving boxes. "I *swear* it was in here . . ."

I shrugged and kept looking for Klawde.

Then I heard clanking noises in the basement, so I went downstairs. They sounded like they were coming from . . . the litter box?

"Klawde?" I said.

The clanking stopped.

Two seconds later, Klawde stepped out of the covered box. For the first time, he had that guilty-dog look.

"Oh, there, there boy!" I said. "You don't have to be embarrassed about using the litter box! Here, I'll clean it for you."

When I went to open the lid, Klawde hissed and swatted at me.

"Ouch, okay!" I said. "*Your* space! I get it. I don't like it when my parents come into my room, either."

Upstairs, I heard Dad at the front door.

"What is in my shoes?" he yelled. "Is this—oh! *Eww!* **Gross!** KLAWDE!"

CHAPTER 16

The return of the boy-Human interrupted my work, and I was forced to bury what I had done under the sand and make myself look innocent.

For the rest of the day, I observed the Humans more closely, trying to understand their ways.

One oddity was how they ate. Why did they use metal tools and weapons to bring their food *up* to their mouths rather than just bringing their mouths *down* to the plate? Could they be so stupid that they never thought of it?

It dawned on me that perhaps such behavior—as well as the lack of technology in the fortress—was not the state of all Humankind but of these *particular* Humans.

I had discovered several other disappointing facts about them:

1. They were not warlords, or warriors, or soldiers of any kind.

2. The weapons packs they carried out of the fortress were not, in fact, weapons packs. They were filled with snacks.

3. Their fortress was not a fortress. It was a mere dwelling. A *home*.

4. They were not all "it"s. The one with long fur on the head was a female. The other two were males. I don't know why it is so hard to tell them apart when it is so easy with cats.

The last fact wasn't actually disappointing, but a point of zoological interest. The first three, however, had me thinking that maybe my Humans were not the best examples of their species. Perhaps other, **stronger** Humans had better technology. Like an intergalactic teleporter.

To find out, I needed to escape.

CHAPTER 17

Tuesday Morning.

I was barely awake yet, but Mom handed me a granola bar, shoved me into the Prius, and ten minutes later, she was dumping me off at the Welcome Cabin again.

"Survive!" she called as she pulled away.

I left my phone in the Forbidden Basket and followed the sound of hissing to the Speaking Stump. I don't know who I was less excited to see—Scorpion and his bully pals or our counselor, who was just beginning his morning talk.

"Today we will begin to learn the language of the forest!" Turkey Vulture declared. "Wild animals are one with nature, and they leave both tracks and signs for us to follow. Can someone tell me the difference?"

Cedar's hand shot up. "Tracks are footprints, and signs are everything else," she said. "Like claw marks on a tree, or a big pile of bear scat."

"Excellent," Turkey Vulture said. "And we must pay attention to both. Now, comrades, follow me!"

We marched off into the woods, and pretty soon I was so turned around I had no idea where we were.

"If you get lost in a forest, you might walk around in endless circles and NEVER get out. But if you find one of *these*, you are saved!" Turkey Vulture pointed to a narrow dirt track worn into the ground. "A deer path always goes somewhere, because deer—unlike humans— never go in circles, and they never get lost."

He led us even deeper into the forest, and then told us to each find a deer trail and use it to get back to the stump. Everyone found one right away.

Except me. I was lost and alone within minutes.

After wandering around for what seemed like forever, feeling stupid and scared, I finally stumbled back to the group. Turkey Vulture was on the Speaking Stump in the middle of a lecture about bird language, and everybody had their deer ears on.

"See? I told you all Rat would *eventually* find his way," Turkey Vulture said cheerfully.

"Welcome back," Cedar whispered.

Turkey Vulture began to whistle in high, short bursts, and then he made some cute peeping noises. "You have just heard the sound of a brown creeper and a common yellowthroat!" he told us. "Most people think birdsong is just pretty music, but it is in fact the sound of greetings, courtship, and warnings! Birds are forest messengers, and even their silence tells us something. Can anyone tell me why you don't hear this much birdsong in your little yards at home?" Turkey Vulture asked.

"Not enough trees?" one kid said.

"Too many cars?" another guessed.

"Lawnmowers!" Steve said.

Turkey Vulture nodded thoughtfully. "These are not stupid theories," he said. "But there is one culprit—one vicious predator—that is most to blame."

His sharp eyes swept over us, but no one dared to guess.

"**Cats!**" Turkey Vulture exclaimed. "Wherever they roam, they hunt and murder songbirds. In fact, the domesticated house cat is the only living creature *more* destructive than human beings!" Turkey Vulture's voice grew cold. "If human beings truly cared about nature, they would stop letting these savage, evil beasts out of their homes!"

Klawde—evil? Now that was ridiculous.

"If only *cats* would become an endangered species!" Turkey Vulture cried happily. "Because on that day, my

friends, the songs of the birds would be joyful indeed."
Then he hopped off the Speaking Stump and danced
around, making a lot of chirping, trilling noises.

I turned to Steve. "Our counselor's crazy," I said.

It made me want to run home and see my kitty cat
right now.

If only I knew the way.

CHAPTER 18

I watched the Humans disappear in their tank. (Which—*sigh*—was just a motorized go-cart with no rocket-launching weaponry whatsoever.)

Leaping down from the window, I went to the front portal. Through careful study, I discovered that it worked on a simple lever. All I had to do was reach up, pull it down, and—**HA!**—I was free!

Recent surveillance of this zone had revealed the existence of *more* Earth cats, and I hoped one of them would know which of the local Humans had the best technology.

Across the road, I'd spotted a flabby, gray-striped tabby who never left one particular window. He appeared stuck to it.

I had low hopes for that one.

In the fortress behind mine, however, lived an orange cat who came and went from her house at will through a push entrance specifically designed for felines. Here, at last, was *some* evidence of technological advancement.

I hurried toward the swinging cat-size door. I pushed against it as I had seen the orange cat do, but nothing happened. I pushed harder with my head. Still nothing.

Did it work off a retinal scan? DNA imaging? This was sophisticated technology indeed!

I waited in a nearby bush until the orange cat came out for her morning exercises.

"Greetings, feline sister!" I said, exiting the bush.

"MROW!" she said. She blinked dumbly at me. "MROW?"

Oh no—not *this* again!

CHAPTER 19

Tuesday Afternoon.

We had been told not to pack lunches because food would be provided. This turned out to be very misleading.

"When you know how to forage, the forest will feed you!" Turkey Vulture declared.

He showed us how to search out berries, wild garlic, chicory, and cattails. The plants weren't that hard to find, but they mostly tasted like grass clippings.

Steve did *not* listen to the part about how to pick and prepare stinging nettles—a lesson he learned painfully—while Cedar called me over to see what she had found under a fallen log. It looked like rice, which I had no idea grew under logs.

Then the rice started to move.

"Excellent find!" Turkey Vulture cried happily. "Grubs, beetles, and insect larvae are a vital part of the wilderness diet!"

He then popped a handful of wriggling white things into his mouth. "Remember that it's not about taste. It's about *survival*!"

If this was survival, I'd rather die of starvation.

When we got back to the Speaking Stump, Turkey Vulture said it was time to choose our packs.

"Our what?" I asked Cedar.

"Our nature teams," she said.

"Why do we need teams?"

"For Survival Night," she said. "Without a pack, you wouldn't last five minutes."

"You mean in the game, right?" I said. *"Right?"*

Cedar just smiled at me as she nibbled on a cattail tuber.

I was afraid no one would want to pick me, but when Turkey Vulture asked Cedar to choose her pack, she pointed at me and Steve.

"Interesting choices," Turkey Vulture said skeptically.

Then Turkey Vulture asked Scorpion who was in his pack.

"Snake and Newt," Scorpion said, pointing to the two kids next to him. Snake was tall and skinny, and Newt was short and freckled, with long, stringy braids. Neither of them looked friendly.

"A bunch of coldbloods, eh?" Turkey Vulture said.

Scorpion nodded. "We were here on this planet first, and we'll be here last." They high-fived.

Turkey Vulture smiled. "I like your spirit, as well as your forest names. But are scorpions indigenous to our area?"

"No, they're from the desert!" I called out. "Elba's more of a temperate rain forest, so scorpions are actually out of place here." I was so excited I finally knew something. Thank you, fifth-grade ecology unit!

"Rat, you may not be as ignorant as I assumed," Turkey Vulture said. "I think the Rat Pack's chances just improved."

Now Cedar and Steve high-fived *me*, and I was feeling pretty good until I saw the death-ray eyes Scorpion was sending my way.

Great. I hadn't made a real friend here yet, but I'd managed to make an enemy.

CHAPTER 20

"MROW!"

It was the same strange word the cats in the prison market had spoken. But what could it mean?

"Miss, please," I said slowly. "My name is Wyss-Kuzz, Lord High Emperor of Planet Lyttyrboks, and I seek answers about the Humans and their technology."

"Mrow?" she said.

No matter how I tried to communicate, she repeated that one word. "Mrow! Mrow? Mrowwww!"

She must have some sort of brain damage. Maybe the swinging door had hit her in the head one too many times.

I had no choice but to approach the Flabby Tabby.

I crossed the road and hopped up to the ledge of the Flabby Tabby's window. Immediately, the cat showed his first signs of life. He arched his back, his fur went up, and he began to hiss.

Assassin's Pose!

It warmed my heart. At least these Earth cats were not *all* meek morons!

"Please, feline brother," I said. "I come in peace! I seek information on the carnivorous ogres known as Humans."

"MROW!" he cried. "MROW! MROW!"

Was it possible? Could these Earth felines know only ONE word? A word of utter nonsense, no less? Thousands of years on this dismal planet must have turned the entire feline race stupid. I never would have believed it! *This* was why they had never overthrown the Humans.

They had become even *more* stupid than the Humans!

I was out of options. I knew I needed to learn

everything I could about the ogres if I was ever going to leave this wretched planet—and there was only one way to do it.

I would have to invade their brains.

CHAPTER 21

Wednesday.

"Has anyone seen the toaster?" my dad asked at breakfast, helplessly holding two floppy halves of an English muffin. "I really need it."

My mom grinned. "I thought the only thing you needed was your Derek Jeter baseball. Does it not make toast?"

It was strange—it seemed like all our small appliances had gone missing. Of course, I'd watched Dad spend an hour looking for car keys that were in his pocket, but still.

"It's a real mystery," I said. "Why don't I stay home from camp and help unpack everything so we can get to the bottom of it?"

"Nice try, dear," Mom said. "Now get in the car."

At the Speaking Stump, Turkey Vulture was holding forth on today's activity: fishing.

"Using baskets you weave yourselves, you will scoop fish from the stream. Then you will gut, roast, and eat your prey."

I raised my hand.

"Uh, I don't eat meat," I said.

Turkey Vulture looked appalled.

"It's a cultural thing," I said. "My whole family is vegetarian."

This wasn't *totally* true. My mom's family was from Karnataka, and they were all serious vegetarians. But Dad snuck hamburgers more than he'd ever admit. (It was not by chance that we wound up at an In-N-Out Burger that time we got lost.)

Turkey Vulture just sighed and put me on basket-weaving duty.

Scorpion walked by with a spear he'd made from a fallen branch. "You know what they call a vegetarian in the woods?" he said to me. "*Prey*."

Gulp.

Everyone else ate themselves silly at lunch. I was so hungry that when Dad picked me up, I scarfed down a half-eaten pack of bunny crackers that had been in the seat pocket since I was in fourth grade.

Camp had exhausted me, too, and I fell asleep almost as soon as I got home. Then I had the weirdest dream. I was back at camp, and the birds were singing so loudly that I couldn't hear what Turkey Vulture was saying. He started pouring birdseed over my head, and the birds flew down and started *peck peck peck*-ing at me, and . . .

I woke up.

But I *still* felt the pecking, like needles in my scalp. *Ow!*

It was Klawde! He was kneading my head with his paws.

"Mrow?" Klawde said.

His first real *meow*! It was so cute!

The claws digging into my forehead really hurt, though.

CHAPTER 22

I was *just* about to complete the mind-meld technique when the small Human awoke.

Hiss!

"Mrow?" I said, pretending to be an idiot Earth cat.

The ogre fell for my ruse. The fool!

Although I had not finished the mind-meld, I had explored enough of the boy-ogre's brain to learn what I needed to. For one thing, I now knew that I *never* wanted to be inside a Human mind again. The creature's cranium was like a dark cave with no exit! But at least I could now understand the Humans' language and some of their ways.

The young ogre, it turned out, had a name: Raj Banerjee. The long-furred ogre was "Mom," and the big, dull one was "Dad." Depressingly, none of them understood *anything* about technology. They had never even visited another planet!

This, I now knew, was the sad truth of all Humans.

I also learned something else, something truly bizarre: The young ogre "loved" me.

This "love" was an entirely un-feline concept. Was it an emotion, like pride or aggression, or a type of illness?

I suspected the latter.

The most mystifying symptom of this affliction was that one ogre would choose to *serve* another ogre—or animal—that it loved. How impossibly strange these Humans were.

The boy-Human placed his bald paw on my head and scratched gently at my ears. Surprisingly, I did not mind this.

Then it struck me.

The boy-ogre had opposable thumbs! This meant

that he would be able to help me build my teleporter.

And since he suffered from this love affliction, he would do my bidding without question.

Purrrr.

CHAPTER 23

Friday Evening.

It was 9:00 p.m., and Week 1 of the most miserable experience of my life was finally over. I actually *limped* into my room and locked the door.

Klawde was sleeping on my pillow.

"You are so lucky you're a cat," I said, crawling into bed and pulling the covers up to my chin. "You get to lie around the house all day while *I* have to go to psycho survival camp."

Klawde leaped to the window ledge and did his furry gargoyle thing.

"I thought *yesterday* was the worst. We had to run up and down the mountain five times and do tree-branch pull-ups. Then there was the boulder-rolling." I rubbed my blisters. "*The Forest Olympics*, Turkey Vulture called it. After that, he had us whittle spears, which was cool until Steve sat on mine and broke it. And Scorpion kept pretending that *I* was the deer-hide target."

Klawde flicked his tail, hopped down from the window, and started pawing at the door.

"You can't leave, Klawde," I said, "because I have to tell you about *today*. Turkey Vulture said we couldn't wear shoes anymore and made us put them in the Forbidden Basket. He calls walking barefoot *earthing* and says humans have done it since the beginning of time. 'Earthing will put you in touch with the natural polarity of the planet and allow you to tap into the earth's energy,' he told us.

"That made it sound like we were getting a superpower, which would've been cool. But rocks are *sharp*, and do you have any idea how many different kinds of plants have thorns on them?"

For some reason, Klawde was now jumping at the door lock and doing that crazy, tortured yowling of his.

"That sounds like the pain *I* feel. I asked Turkey Vulture for some Band-Aids, but he said that cuts were a minor inconvenience on the way to getting our *forest feet*."

I scratched at one of my thousand bug bites.

"The last thing he told us was how we should enjoy our weekend, 'For after Survival Night, your lives will NEVER BE THE SAME!' Can you believe that? Crazy, right?"

Klawde was just staring at me now, his tail swishing.

He looked about as sympathetic as my mom had been at dinner when I'd asked her if I could skip the second week of camp. She'd told me to forget it.

"Raj *has* tried it for a whole week, dear," Dad pointed out.

But that didn't matter to her. "We *never* give up," Mom said. "A Banerjee ALWAYS finishes what she starts!"

"But, Mom, I'm not a *she*!"

"That's not the point."

In other words, I was going back.

I hopped off the bed and put my face close to Klawde's.

"I just wish there was no Camp Eclipse and no Oregon and I could go home to Brooklyn!" I said. "Life is too *hard* here!"

And then Klawde said something.

In *English*.

CHAPTER 24

I was trapped! Trapped in that locked room with the boy-Human and his incessant, pathetic complaining!

I would rather have my fur plucked out hair by hair than listen to one more word. I had to say something.

"Will you stop whining and **SHUT UP!**"

Well, maybe *that* wasn't what I should have said.

The Human's jaw dropped open. He backed away from me.

"Klawde?" he said. "Did you just *speak* to me?"

There was terror in his voice. I liked that.

I considered keeping up my charade and saying "Mrow." He'd think he was going mad—a delicious idea!—but I needed this boy-Human's help if I ever wanted to get back home.

I had to do some fast talking.

"Raj Banerjee of Earth," I said in my most majestic tone. "I am not of this planet. I come from a highly advanced world on the other side of the universe."

The Human now appeared unable to speak. I was not sure if this was due to awe, fear, or basic idiocy.

"I am not, however, your average space-cat. On my planet, I led a glorious invasion—er, I mean, *revolution*—a glorious revolution which united all cats together in . . . in . . . in peace—yes, yes, **peace**!" I purred. "I ruled my planet as a kind and benevolent warlord."

The Human just blinked at me.

"Okay . . . ," the boy-ogre said slowly. "So my cat is an . . . *alien warlord*?"

"A *kind* alien warlord."

"A kind alien warlord *cat*."

His puny brain appeared to be processing this information. Could he possibly be gullible enough to buy it?

"That's the coolest thing **ever**!" he said, leaping back to life. "I can't believe it! I'm the luckiest kid in the WORLD!"

Then the boy-Human began blurting out annoying questions.

"How can you talk?" "How did you get here?" "Why did you leave your planet?" "Are there people where you live?" "What about dogs?" "Is there gravity?" "How many suns do you have?" "Can I see your spaceship?" "Have you ever seen a black hole?" "Why did you come to Earth?" "Have you been to Mars?"

"Enough!" I said. "My right-paw cat BETRAYED me, and I was sent to this planet in *exile*!"

"Oh." The boy-Human looked at me curiously. "Hey, so what's your alien name?"

"Alien name? My *real* name . . . ," I said, "is Wyss-Kuzz!"

"Awww, that's so cute! Your name is *Whiskers*!"

"No no no—not *Whiskers*!" These Humans with their fat, bloated tongues—they couldn't pronounce anything correctly! "It's Wyss-Kuzz! **Wyss-KUZZ!**"

The boy-ogre shrugged. "Sounds like *Whiskers* to me."

I had vaporized ambassadors and kings for lesser insults, but as I needed this Human's help to get home, I made an exception.

CHAPTER 25

Saturday.

When I woke up that morning, I was sure it had all
been a dream. I immediately went to look for Klawde, but
he wasn't in the kitchen, or staring out the front window,
or napping in any of his usual spots. Where *was* he?

I'd have looked more, but first I had to go to the
bathroom. I opened the door.

"Ex-CUSE me!"

Klawde was sitting on the
toilet reading the *Wall
Street Journal.*

"Oh, sorry!" I said, and quickly shut the door.

Wow. My cat really *was* an *alien*! Who **talked**!! And could **read**! And used the **toilet**!

HOW COOL!!!

And not only that—he had ruled a whole planet! He was a warlord. But a *kind* warlord.

A Kind Alien Warlord Cat!

It was all true!

I had the best pet **EVER**!

And I had *soooo* many more questions.

"What kind of special alien powers do you have?" I whispered through the door. "Are you as powerful as *Americaman*?" I asked. "What is life like on your cat planet? Is there oxygen there? Trees? Mice? Houses?"

I waited for him to answer, but he hissed at me for some reason.

"How did you unite your planet?" I went on. "How big is your planet? How do cats fight there?

With weapons? Do they fight in *space*?!"

I'd been obsessed with space ever since I went to the planetarium on a second-grade class trip.

"Is there life on *lots* of other planets?"

"How do you travel through space?"

"What is it *like* to travel through space?"

"Can *I* travel through space?"

I heard another hiss. And then the toilet flushing.

"I can't wait to tell all my friends back in Brooklyn!" I said. "They won't believe I have an *alien* cat!"

The door swung open to reveal Klawde standing in the doorway.

"NO!" he said, swishing his tail. "My existence on your planet must be a secret! Tell **no one**!"

"What?" I said, confused. "Why?"

Klawde leaped to the top of the hall bookshelf and was now at eye level with me.

"TELL . . . NO . . . ONE!" he said fiercely.

"Okay, *okay*," I said, putting my hands up.

Klawde fluffed up his tail. "We are dealing with a very *serious* matter."

"I won't tell anybody—I promise."

"I am referring to something else now." He licked a paw and gazed straight into my eyes. "I need your help. Will you *help* me, Raj?"

"Of course," I said. "I'll do anything!"

He purred.

"I need you to help me build a teleporter," he said. "So I can return to . . . Lyttyrboks!"

CHAPTER 26

The boy-ogre wore his most senseless expression yet.

"Litter box?" he said. "But you have the litter box we bought you right here, with the snap-on lid and everything!"

This time, it took all the strength I possessed not to fling myself at his idiotically happy face.

I brushed my whiskers with a paw and composed myself.

"Perhaps it is best for you *not* to attempt to pronounce the sophisticated sounds of Lytt—er, *my planet*," I said.

The look on the boy-ogre's face told me that, at last, some of the synapses in his brain were firing.

"Wait, what are you saying?" he said. "That you want to go *back* to your planet?"

Or maybe the synapses weren't firing after all.

"Of course I want to go back to my planet!" I cried.

Suddenly the boy-Human was no longer happy. In fact, he looked as if he'd been wounded. Could this have something to do with his strange love disease?

"You want to *leave*?" he said. "But you just got here!"

I had to calm the ogre down in order to secure his help. So I lied.

"It is not for *myself* that I must return home. Why, I would *love* to stay here on this . . . this . . . WONDERFUL planet." I felt another hairball coming on. "But I have to return home so I can reconq—er, that is— **rescue** all the poor cats I left behind."

"But you're my only real friend here," the ogre said.

Then drops of water began leaking out of the Human's eyes and sliding down his furless face. What was *wrong* with this creature?

"I want to go with you," he wailed, wiping away the eye fluid.

"Oh, how I wish you *could* come with me," I said.

I was lying again, of course.

But then I thought, YES! Come *with* me. Imagine!

Having a giant at my side to help me reconquer

Lyttyrboks. I'd be **INVINCIBLE**! I could see the terrified

look on General Ffangg's face now!!

Purr.

For someone with such limited intelligence, the idea of space travel would be terrifying, of course. But what if I could make his own planet seem *worse* than terrifying? After all, our mind-meld had told me much about the boy-ogre's prospects here—and they did not look good.

"Oh, how wonderful it would be if you could come with me! You would love my planet!" I said. "But you have your excellent *survival* camp to complete. And there's this new *city* to get to know, and a whole new *school* you must attend! I'm sure you will be *very* popular. No doubt all the older child-Humans will be *very, very welcoming.*"

The little Human looked like *he* was about to cough up a hairball.

This was my greatest evil plan yet! If I could convince him to come along, the monstrous boy-ogre would be my one-soldier army! I would string General Ffangg up by his tail, and the Most High Throne would once again be mine!

Swish, purr, purrrrr!

CHAPTER 27

Sunday.

Disappointed was not the word.

Disappointed was when the Knicks lost a game.

Disappointed was when the ice-cream shop ran out of chocolate.

Disappointed was when I left my new stack of comics on the subway.

But *this*? Learning that my pet was a Kind Alien Warlord Cat, and the *next* day finding out that he was leaving? That was a billion times more disappointing than any disappointment **ever**!

And what was worse, I had to *help* him leave!

"Human! Pay attention!" Klawde said. "Align the diode with the capacitor and then move the magnetron seven degrees left."

"Huh?"

Klawde sighed and shook his head at me.

We were in the basement, surrounded by microwave parts, blender pieces, hair-dryer bits, and DVD-player fragments.

I'd finally learned where all our appliances were going: straight into Klawde's otherwise unused litter box. Or—as he called it—his "work station."

Thankfully, he'd let me move the operation from the litter box into the shop in the basement. It had a bunch of tools the previous owners had left behind, and it was the one room my parents never went into. We'd been working for *hours* now.

"Yes, line it up like that," Klawde said. "No, back to the right a bit . . . use your thumbs!"

"Sorry!"

Building with Klawde was kind of fun, as long as

I didn't think about what I was making: a device that would take my pet away.

Klawde did yell a lot, though. He got especially mad when I couldn't follow his written directions.

"Point 17K states you must make the energetic particle radiation density buffer bypass the aft tactical resonance coil," Klawde said. "How much *clearer* could it be?!"

The problem was that I couldn't understand his alien claw-writing. It just looked like scratched cardboard to me.

As I unthreaded the tiny screws from the density buffer—whatever that was—I asked Klawde if he missed his home planet.

"Of course I miss it!" Klawde said. "It is a place of marvels beyond Human comprehension, and I ruled it all with an iron paw! Cats trembled when I spoke! My minions—"

"I thought you said you were a *nice* warlord," I said.

"Oh, yes," Klawde said. "Just kidding. Have I told you about the Purring Palace?"

While I worked on the teleporter, Klawde described the wonders of his home planet.

"I tell you, I miss each and every one of the eighty-seven moons of Lyttyrboks," Klawde said. "I even miss the toxic yellow atmosphere of Number Seventy-Four."

"And I miss all of Brooklyn," I said. "Even the toxic green water of the Gowanus Canal."

"Human," Klawde said with a sigh, "we are *both* in exile."

CHAPTER 28

The Humans have a primitive information-sharing system they call "the internet," which we used to find parts I needed for the teleporter. To purchase them, the boy-ogre entered a series of numbers into a touch screen and said, "It's a good thing Dad never checks his credit card statements."

I did not know what that meant.

Once the Human finished placing the order, I went to the front portal.

"What are you doing?" he asked.

"I am going to receive the parts." How dumb *was* he?

"But they won't be here for two days," the boy-Human said.

"Two days!" I said. "What kind of instant ordering takes *two days*?"

The aggravation of this primitive world!

"What do you need a vacuum chamber for, anyway?" the boy-Human asked. "Or a photonic logic gate?"

The young ogre's endless questions bored me, so I took a nap. Despite the delays, we were making progress on the device. I calculated that within four days' time, I would be able to return home.

General Ffangg will rue the day he crossed whiskers with me! I could almost taste my **REVENGE**!!

CHAPTER 29

Monday.

Even by Monday standards, this was a terrible Monday.

I couldn't believe I had to leave my *talking alien cat* to go suffer another week of Camp Eclipse. The week that would end with Survival Night! Honestly, rocketing into space with Klawde sounded *way* less terrifying.

"But it's a game," Mom said at breakfast. "You love games."

"*Board* games, Mom," I said. "Not try-not-to-die games."

I told her that I *refused* to go back for another week.

And then we got in the car.

As the Prius silently glided into the Mount Eclipse parking lot, my heart sank. I left my cell phone and shoes in the Forbidden Basket and made the dreaded walk to the Speaking Stump.

"We begin this week with the Pack Challenges," Turkey Vulture announced excitedly. "They will help prepare you for surviving the apocalypse. For surviving . . . SURVIVAL NIGHT!"

Turkey Vulture looked straight at me.

"Survival Night is *more* than a game," he went on. "Paintball is a game. Dungeons and Dragons is a game. Survival Night is REAL. For twenty-four hours, you will be living in a postapocalyptic world."

Then Turkey Vulture's voice got very soft. "The

year is 2047, and global warming has caused the seas to rise one hundred feet. The world economy has been destroyed. No technology exists! The internet is DEAD!"

I gasped.

"What few humans remain have taken to higher ground, and only those who can adapt will survive. The question you must ask yourself is . . . will *you* be one of them?"

"YES!" Scorpion yelled, and he and the rest of the Cold Bloods cheered. So did Cedar.

"Why are you clapping?" I whispered. "This sounds terrible!"

"It's going to be amazing!" Cedar said. "This is why we *wanted* to come to the camp, Rat!"

"What *we*?" I said. "My mom forced me to come."

Turkey Vulture explained that today's challenge was a race to build a shelter on the top of Mount Eclipse.

"Okay, guys," Cedar said, turning to me and Steve.

"There aren't many trees at the top of the mountain, so we should collect our branches and leaves here at the base. Let's fan out and meet at the top. Now go, go, *go*!"

As I gathered sticks on my own, Newt broke off from the Cold Bloods and came over to me.

"I shouldn't be telling you this, but I was the new kid last year, so I know what it's like," she whispered. "The main path to the summit takes forever. But there's a shortcut." She looked around to see if anyone was listening. "Go across the sword fern meadow and head through the pines. You'll get there way ahead of everyone else!" Then she sprinted off to join the other Cold Bloods.

The sword fern meadow? That was where we foraged for snails. I actually *knew* where that was!

I started running with my armful of sticks and leaves. I sprinted through the meadow and up into the woods. This *was* way faster.

And then I got to the chain-link fence.

A sign read:

PATH TO SUMMIT CLOSED FOR MAINTENANCE

That slimy, rotten Newt! She tricked me!

CHAPTER 30

The boy-Human's inability to focus was needlessly delaying the work he and his thumbs needed to do. He could not stop bellyaching about the military camp he attended.

It seemed that one of his enemies had tricked him into following the wrong course in a war-training exercise, causing Raj's battalion to lose.

"You must declaw this Newt and chop off her tail!" I said.

"But she's a *kid*. She doesn't have claws *or* a tail."

I sighed. Did this Human have *no* imagination? "Then rip all the fur off her head," I said. "Now take the alphaphotonic coil and connect it to the barytrine barrier."

"What?" the boy-Human said.

"Stick those two things together, you fool!"

"Darn it! Now the remote is broken, too!" I heard the father-Human say upstairs. "And what happened to all the *batteries*?" Next came the sound of kitchen drawers slamming.

I feared the father-Human had begun to get suspicious.

"I just don't know what to do," the boy-ogre said. "I let my team down, and without them, I'm all alone in that crazy place. Why did Newt trick me like that?"

I looked firmly at the boy-ogre. "We have a saying on my planet: *All is fair in war!*"

"Oh, we have that saying, too," he said. "Except it's all is fair in *love* and war."

"That's ridiculous," I muttered.

"Klawde, you were the greatest leader your planet ever had. Don't you have any advice for me?"

I sighed. I could see the boy-ogre would be incapable of helping me unless I helped him first. Perhaps I could turn him into an adequate soldier yet.

"We have another saying on my planet," I said. *"He who climbs the highest tree has not the sharpest claws, but the strongest heart!"*

The boy-Human nodded, in awe of this ancient feline wisdom.

Or not. It was impossible to tell what these Humans were thinking with their expressionless faces!

CHAPTER 31

Tuesday.

"I heard you got lost yesterday," Scorpion said. "Did you have to call a cab to get to the summit?"

He and the other Cold Bloods burst out laughing.

"It was that jerk's fault and you *know* it," Cedar said, pointing at Newt, who grinned proudly. "If it wasn't for that trick, we would've built a great shelter."

"Yeah, but you built a brush pile!" Snake said. "Good luck sleeping *there* on Survival Night!"

The flapping and hissing began as Turkey Vulture mounted the Speaking Stump. He picked right back up where he'd left off the day before.

"Imagine, my young survivalists, the seas rising up the slopes of this ancient volcano. Tsunamis wiping away all that you have ever known!" Turkey Vulture said. "Where will *you* go when the great waters rise?"

"Swimming?" Steve said.

"*No,*" Turkey Vulture said, rolling his eyes. "You will take to the **trees**!"

We all looked up.

"The trees will be your safe haven," Turkey Vulture said. "Not only from the seas, but from the predators. Such as hungry packs of rival humans."

Steve raised his hand. "You mean . . . *cannibals?*"

Turkey Vulture nodded. "It is a little-known fact that cannibalism was widespread among many premodern societies." He gave us a toothy grin. "It is a practice that will surely return in the *post*modern world!"

I was starting to wonder if Turkey Vulture *liked* violence and destruction.

I was also beginning to wonder the same thing about Klawde. If all he really wanted was to bring peace to his home planet, why did he keep talking about *making the traitors pay* and *launching a new reign of terror*?

Was it possible that Klawde was *not* a Kind Alien Warlord Cat? That maybe—just maybe—he was an *Evil Alien Warlord Cat*?

Even if he was, though, he was still MY Evil Alien Warlord Cat, and I didn't want him to leave Earth. And if he did, I wanted to go with him.

But I couldn't think about Klawde right now. We were about to have our next challenge.

"If you want to survive," our counselor yelled, "start *climbing*!"

CHAPTER 32

"Here, kitty kitty kitty!"

The father-ogre was trying to lure me onto his lap with some of the dried food pellets.

I approached him boldly.

"OWW!" he said, putting the finger I'd just bitten into his mouth. "Naughty kitty!"

I began to purr. It had been far too long since I injured something.

DING-DONG!

"Now who could *that* be?" the father-ogre said.

He opened the front portal to reveal another hideous Human, this one dressed all in brown. Was it for some kind of military camouflage?

He handed the father-ogre an electronic device. "Sign here for delivery, sir."

"What *is* all this?" the father-Human said, looking at the boxes while he squiggled a stick at the device. "Maybe a new toaster!"

He did not open any of the boxes, however, because he was "going to be late for work," a concept unfamiliar to felines. As soon as he left, I tore into them. Within the packages I found diodes, capacitors, a potentiometer, and more: all the final parts I needed to complete my teleporter.

I also now had the critical parts for my *other* project—a transuniversal communicator.

Although I did not have the boy-Human to assist me, I completed the assembly of this all-important device with ease, pausing for only three brisk naps.

Oh, how I could hardly wait to call home and hear the sweet feline language of Lyttyrboks again!

Once the communicator was functional, I dialed

the *one* servant who had remained loyal to the end: Lieutenant Flooffee-Fyr.

When his face appeared on the screen, his surprise and joy were clear.

CHAPTER 33

Tuesday, Continued.

Turkey Vulture had said that whoever climbed the highest would win the challenge for their team. So the trick wasn't just picking the tallest tree, but the one that was the most climbable. From what I could tell, Cedar, Scorpion, and Newt had picked the best trees, and they were already on their way up.

As for me, I was still on the ground trying to choose. I didn't want to be the one who lost the challenge for our team—*again*. But for once, there was hope.

I'd always been good at climbing, even if it was never exactly in nature. Back home, my local playground had a rock-climbing wall that I loved, and I'd been the best climber in my after-school program at Brooklyn Boulders.

The tree I *really* wanted to climb looked as tall as the Empire State Building, but I couldn't reach even its lowest branches. Then I had an idea.

"Hey, Steve!" I hollered.

Steve was the only other kid still on the ground, having twice fallen out of an oak.

"Can you give me a leg up?"

"No prob," Steve said, and he bent down so I could use his back as a springboard. It worked perfectly.

"Thanks!" I called down from the branches. "Now what about you?"

"I'm about to try to—"

"HE'S ABOUT TO GET SWEPT AWAY BY THE GREATEST TSUNAMI IN RECORDED HISTORY!" hollered Turkey Vulture.

"Climb, Rat! Climb!" shouted Steve, dodging our

counselor, who was now pretending to be a giant tidal wave.

I began to clamber up, plotting the best route as I went. But how high would I need to go to beat the others?

Scorpion I'd get past, no problem. He was already stuck, and shouting out his frustration as branch after branch snapped under his weight. Cedar seemed like she was stuck, too. Newt, however, was already halfway to the sky. The little liar was scaling her pine tree like a ladder.

My hands were sticky with sap, and twigs kept poking me in the eyes. This was *way* harder than scaling a wall studded with fake plastic rocks. But I kept going.

I passed Scorpion and Cedar and was now almost as high as Newt, who had gotten caught in a tangle of vines. Maybe I *could* win!

And that's when I looked down. Which was a major mistake.

I was *way* higher than the Mt. Everest wall at Brooklyn Boulders. And there was no padded mat at the bottom! What was I **thinking**?

I froze in terror.

Turkey Vulture yelled, "Rat stopped! The Cold Bloods win!"

"No, wait!" Cedar cried from somewhere below. "He isn't done yet! Come on, Rat!"

I wanted to climb higher so badly, but I couldn't move.

Then the words of Klawde came ringing into my ears:

He who climbs the highest tree has not the sharpest claws, but the strongest heart.

I felt myself moving again. My hands reached up and my feet found higher branches, and pretty soon I had run out of tree. I was swaying in the crown of my tree, able to see the tops of all the other ones below me. I was the highest!

"He won!" Cedar shouted. "Rat won!"

I *did* win! It felt amazing! Like I was a *hero*!

There was only one problem: How the heck was I going to get back down?

CHAPTER 34

"OH GREAT LORD AND MASTER," Flooffee-Fyr
mewed. "HOW THRILLED I AM TO SEE THAT YOU
ARE WELL! THANK THE EIGHTY-SEVEN MOONS!"

"You have no idea the indignities I have suffered,"
I told my loyal servant. "But they will be nothing
compared to what my *enemies* will suffer! Tell me,
Flooffee, are the felines of Lyttyrboks clamoring for my
return?"

"Well . . . ," Flooffee-Fyr said slowly. "They *have*
stopped burning you in effigy."

"Do they yet cower under the tyranny of General
Ffangg? Are they desperate to return to the days of my
iron-pawed rule?"

"Ummmm . . . ," Flooffee-Fyr said. He scratched at
his ear with a hind paw. "Most cats actually seem pretty,

uh, happy these days? General Ffangg made furcare a universal right, and everyone is super-excited about the unlimited free trips to the exuviating parlor."

"He's trying to buy them off! It's an insult! The good felines of Lyttyrboks must see through his sneaky ways!"

"Well . . . ," Flooffee-Fyr said. "He's *also* granted free lifetime claw trimming. And he planted a billion new trees to replace the ones you burned in the last war."

"So, in other words, the time is RIPE for my return!"

"To be honest, sir, I think—"

"Silence!" I cried. Flooffee-Fyr had never understood politics, and I didn't have time to explain it to him.

What I needed was help testing the teleporter, which I had completed that morning after receiving the final components from the delivery ogre. As for an object to send across the universe, I had chosen what appeared to be a combat training ball that I found under a glass jar in the humans' main parlor. It was white with red stitching and had the name of some Human—a *Derek Jeter*—scribbled on it. Probably the father-ogre had stolen it from this Derek Jeter.

Naturally, I approved of such behavior. But I would now steal it from *him*!

I placed the ball in the teleporter under the beam of protophotonic gamma flash. With a press of the button, there was a burst of green light.

And Derek Jeter's ball was gone.

Moments later, I watched it enter Lyttyrboks's atmosphere in another burst of green light. It hovered in the air for a moment, and then it dropped down on top of Flooffee-Fyr's head.

"*Ow!*" Flooffee cried.

I pinned my ears in disgust at his whimpering.

"Show it to me," I commanded.

"Right here," he said, lowering his head. "See the lump?"

"No, you fool," I said. "The *ball*!"

"Oh," Flooffee-Fyr said, and held it up. The ball was in perfect condition.

Success!

Still, Flooffee-Fyr insisted that we test the teleporter on something living before I risked *my* precious life in it.

"I have some expendable Humans handy," I said.

"No," Flooffee-Fyr said, still rubbing behind his ear. "We need something closer to your size and genetic makeup. Are there any Earth cats you could use?"

Hmmm . . .

CHAPTER 35

Tuesday Afternoon.

"Klawde! Klawde! Where *are* you?"

I couldn't wait to tell him how I'd won a challenge thanks to his advice! I finally found him in the garage, but I hadn't even gotten to the good part when he cut me off.

"Silence! Enough about your pointless life!" Klawde said. "*Er*, I mean your very IMPORTANT problems— because I have exciting news! The teleporter works and is ready to be tested on a *living* being."

I was about to ask what we would test it on when I heard, "Hello? Is anybody in there?"

It was Lindy, the one-grade-younger girl who lived across the street.

"Oh, it's just you," Lindy said. "I thought I heard *two* voices."

"That was the radio," I said, thinking quickly.

"What radio?" she said.

"Umm . . ."

"OOOH! Is this your kitty?" She bent down to pet Klawde.

"Don't do that," I said, grabbing her arm. "He's not that kind of cat."

"*What* kind of cat?"

"The petting kind."

Klawde swished his tail and growled a little.

"Oh, that's terrible! My cat, Chad, just *loves* to be picked up and petted and hugged! He's really smart, too!"

"HAH!" Klawde said.

"What a weird meow he has!" Lindy said.

"My dad thinks he's part Siamese."

"Oh, I think Chad's part Siamese, too!" she said. Then she looked at Klawde. "They even look a bit alike. I mean, Chad is a *little* fuzzier around the belly, but they're basically the same size."

For some reason, Klawde started purring very loudly.

"So, what are you doing tomorrow?" Lindy asked. "My mom's taking me and my friends to Wanda's Waterslide World and there's still room in the minivan if you wanna come."

"I wish I could. But I have to go to Camp Eclipse."

"Ohhh, you go to Camp Apocalypse!" she said. "I've heard *all* about that camp. My brother's friend went last year. He said that on the last night of the camp, a kid died!" She shrugged. "Anyway, bye!"

I gulped as Lindy walked away.

I thought about the teleporter in the basement, ready to rocket Klawde across the universe. Maybe there was room in it for me.

"This sounds like a most excellent camp!" Klawde said. "I really do not know why you complain about it so much."

CHAPTER 36

"Here, *kitty kitty kitty* . . . Yummy treats for you, Flabby Tabby!"

These "cat treats" were an abomination, but they had clearly been engineered to appeal to the weak constitutions of Earth felines.

Flabby Tabby gobbled them up, one after the other, like a fotobarastic particle vacuum.

He followed the trail across the street, into the house, and down the stairs, right into the teleporter. It was really too easy.

As Flabby Tabby sat there, chewing his final treat with a stupid expression on his face, I pressed the button, closed my eyes against the green flash, and . . .

ZAP!

Flabby was gone!

I reached for my communicator. "Flooffee-Fyr! Come in, Flooffee-Fyr!"

My loyal minion's face appeared on-screen. "Greetings, commander!"

"Have you received the package?"

"The what?"

And then, in the background, I saw the green flash.

"It just arrived!" Flooffee-Fyr confirmed. "Test successful, oh lord and commander!"

Purr!

Flooffee turned to Flabby Tabby. "Welcome to your ancestral home of Lyttyrboks, Earth cat!"

"MROW," said Flabby.

Flooffee-Fyr cocked his head. "Space traveler, can you understand me?"

"MROW!" said Flabby.

And then Flabby Tabby started cleaning a part of his body that we normally do not clean in public. And certainly not with our tongues!

Flooffee's horrified face appeared close up in the communicator screen. "Lord High Emperor, I have terrible news. The journey to Lyttyrboks has scrambled his brain!"

"No, *all* Earth cats are like that," I said. "With giant ogres feeding and housing them, they had no need to think or act. They *devolved*."

"That is very unfortunate," Flooffee-Fyr said,

holding up a paw to shield his eyes from the spectacle.

"Run some tests on him," I said. "Make sure the teleporter did not do additional damage to his weak brain."

Flooffee-Fyr saluted and signed off.

I had just a few final preparations before I could leave this godforsaken planet. I could smell victory. I had not yet told Flooffee, but I was expecting to have a secret weapon by my side! A HUMAN weapon.

CHAPTER 37

Wednesday.

"Tomorrow is the night you've all been waiting for!"
Turkey Vulture said as he handed us each a piece of bark.
On it was a list of what we needed for Survival Night.

Water bottle

Flashlight

Pocketknife

Courage

Bandages

"Today shall be a day of rest and reflection," our
counselor said with unusual calmness. "Of strolling
along the forest's paths, of gathering and foraging."

That didn't sound so bad.

But Turkey Vulture wasn't done.

"Because beginning tomorrow, the last glaciers have melted. The waters have risen three hundred feet. In the entire world, there are now only islands of land." Here he stopped for a . . . *dramatic* . . . pause.

"Like . . . *this* . . . volcano!"

Everyone gasped.

"I just love his stories!" Cedar whispered to me.

"But it's not just a story! Not to *him*!" I said. "My neighbor told me a kid died last year!"

"What*? Really?*" Steve said.

"That can't be true," Cedar said.

"How can you be so sure?" I said. "We still don't even know what the game *is*."

"I'll tell you babies what it is!" Scorpion said. "It's Hide-or-Get-Eaten times a *million*!"

"And when it's done," Newt added, "you're gonna

wish you'd never been born!"

Snake just stared at us and dragged his finger slowly across his neck.

Later, as we foraged and fixed up our shelter, Cedar tried to cheer Steve and me up.

"Remember, it's just like Turkey Vulture said—nature is our friend!"

What he'd *actually* said was that nature was all-powerful and couldn't care less if humans went extinct, but I didn't bother to correct her.

In the car ride back, I didn't even talk to my mother. I felt like I was going to throw up.

A kid died last year, Lindy had said.

And then I saw her—Lindy. Mom turned down our street and there she was, putting up a poster on the telephone pole in front of our house.

When her family got home from the waterslide park, Lindy told me, the cat was gone. Somehow, a

window had been left open.

"Chad will never survive outside!" she said, starting to cry. "He's never even *been* outside! And he's NEUTERED!"

"I know how he feels," I said. "About not surviving outside, I mean."

And I *did* mean it. I really didn't think I would— not for a whole night, and definitely not with the Cold Bloods out to get me.

I tried to talk to Klawde about it, but all he cared about was the teleporter.

"It worked!" Klawde purred, rubbing against it. "I sent a live animal across the universe!"

"What animal?" I said. "Wait a minute—Lindy's cat is missing. You didn't . . ."

"What *kind* of a feline do you think I am?" Klawde said, offended. "It was a mouse!"

I looked at the teleporter that I'd helped build. "Is it powerful enough to send something bigger than a cat across the universe?" I said.

CHAPTER 38

By the time the boy-Human returned from battle camp, I had received excellent news: The Flabby Tabby was completely healthy, morbid obesity aside. My departure was now at hand.

Even *more* excellent news came from the boy-ogre himself. He was on the claw's edge of coming with me! All he needed was a bit more encouragement.

"And we could leave *tomorrow?*" he asked.

"Absolutely!" I said.

"And you would send me back home *whenever* I wanted?"

"Of course!"

As the young Human went off to his sleeping chamber, my tail swished in pleasure.

My evil scheme was working PERFECTLY!

In the morning, the boy-ogre came to me in the underground bunker he referred to as the basement.

"Okay," he said. "I want to go with you."

What joy! This giant would render me **invincible**! I could taste final victory! I had to call Flooffee-Fyr and tell him the excellent news.

But before I could do anything, there was that infernal sound from the front portal.

DING-DONG!

"Raj!" the father-Human called. "It's for you!"

CHAPTER 39

Thursday Morning.

I'd barely slept all night. This was the biggest decision of my life. By morning, I'd decided that the chance to travel to another planet—a planet of cats!— was too awesome to miss.

Especially since it meant I'd be missing Survival Night.

But just as I told Klawde I would go with him, the doorbell rang.

Who could it be? At 7:00 a.m.? I went to the front door and found Cedar and Steve on the porch.

"*This* guy showed up at my house an hour ago," Cedar said, pointing at Steve.

"I couldn't sleep!" Steve said. "Every time I closed

my eyes, I thought about the RISING SEAS! And the CANNIBALS!"

"I keep telling him all that disaster stuff is just part of the game, but he won't believe me," Cedar said.

My dad appeared behind me with a cup of coffee. "It's so nice you've made friends, son!"

Friends? I wanted to say. *They're just two kids I've been doomed to die with!*

Except that I'd found a way *not* to die. And maybe I could save them, too.

"Can you guys keep a secret?" I whispered. "A *big* secret?"

They both nodded yes.

"Come on," I said, and led them down to the basement.

"Hey, what's that awful noise?" Cedar said. "It sounds like a baboon getting his nose hairs ripped out."

It was Klawde, of course. He was in his covered

litter box, using his communicator to tell his most trusted lieutenant I was joining him.

"That's my cat," I said. "*He's* the secret."

"What do you mean?" Cedar asked.

"My cat," I said, "is an **alien**."

"Huh?" Steve said.

Cedar looked really confused. "Raj, are you feeling okay?"

Klawde stepped out of the litter box and saw everyone staring at him. His tail swished.

"And not only is he an alien," I went on, "he's a *warlord*. He conquered his entire planet, and *I'm* going there to help him reunite the cats of planet Lyttyrboks!"

"Warlord?" Cedar said.

"*Litter box?*" Steve said.

"No, it's not pronounced that way—oh, never mind. We're leaving *today*."

Cedar touched my arm. "Rat, you're not making sense. Are you okay?"

"We built a teleporter." I pointed to the tangle of metal and wire in the corner. "You can both come and help us! Then you won't have to go to Survival Night!"

Cedar and Steve looked back and forth between me and the teleporter. Then Steve burst out laughing.

"I don't know what's funnier," he said. "The thought of you riding through space in that pile of scrap metal or the idea that your cat is an alien!"

But I could *prove* it.

"Go ahead, Klawde," I said. "Speak. Tell them who you really are!"

Klawde looked at me, and then at Cedar and Steve. He blinked, and said one word:

"Mrow?"

CHAPTER 40

After the two other child-Humans left, shaking their heads, my Human turned to me.

"Why did you *do* that?" he demanded. "Now they think I'm crazy! I thought you *wanted* humans to come help you reconquer your planet! You could've had two more!"

"Raj," I said, "I have *heard* what has gone on in this room! I see that you are no longer alone in this place."

"Well, I guess they're *kind* of my friends . . ."

"They are more important than friends!" I said, scolding him. "They are your comrades-in-arms. Your partners in battle! And that is a bond even stronger than *littermates*!"

He did not look convinced.

"You must not shrink from tonight's war. Reach

down beneath your fur—or whatever that is covering your hideous body—and bring out the inner feline: the **battle cat**!" I cried. "As I said to my troops before the War of Skratshink Poast, it is better to die ten thousand deaths than turn tail and run! An army need not be stronger—only smarter! And crueler!"

The Human was clearly moved by my words.

"But what about going to Lyttyrboks?" he said.

"It is with a heavy heart that I have to tell you this, Raj Banerjee, but I can**not** take you across the universe!" I said. "I see now that your fight is *here,* on Earth. You are needed on this planet—for Survival Night, and beyond."

The Human was confused and disappointed, and it seemed that his eyes might leak again. He made me promise that I wouldn't leave before he returned. *If* he returned.

I said that I would wait for him, and wished him luck.

He paused at the door.

"Thanks," he said. "It makes me happy to know that you really care about me."

From the window, I watched as he climbed into the family go-cart, which would transport him to the battle's frontlines. I wondered if he would survive.

It seemed unlikely.

I was just relieved that he had believed all the nonsense I had told him. I needed him out of my fur so I could use the teleporter—alone!

There had been a sudden and unavoidable change of plans. While the boy-Human was talking to the other child-Humans, I'd called Flooffee-Fyr to tell him the good news. But Flooffee had informed me that Humans were too big to use the teleporter.

"If you try," Flooffee-Fyr said, "the Human will explode, and his molecules will be scattered across a billion light-years of space like so many subatomic specks of dust and gore."

"So you're saying it's worth a shot?"

"No," Flooffee-Fyr had said. "Not unless you want a very messy teleporter."

CHAPTER 41

Thursday.

Up on the Speaking Stump, Turkey Vulture was
hissing and flapping with more energy than ever.

"Today is the DAY!" he cried. "Here at the top of
Mount Eclipse, the last threads of civil society have
broken down. All remaining humans have divided into

clans and retreated into the woods, where they fight each other over what precious few resources remain."

"Can I hold your hand?" Steve whispered to me.

Turkey Vulture cupped his hands at the sides of his head. "When you put on your deer ears, you can hear it. Humanity's final, gasping breaths!"

I looked over at Cedar, and even *she* looked a little nervous.

Then Turkey Vulture explained the rules of the game.

"You are truly in nature now! Together with your packs, you will live off what you have foraged and spend the night in your shelter. But that is not all," he said with a grin. "You will also be hunting . . . *each other*."

Steve gasped. Or maybe that was me.

"You will sneak through the dark woods on your forest feet," Turkey Vulture said, hopping off the Speaking Stump and tiptoeing around us. "Then you will lie in wait for your rival humans. When one appears, you *attack*!"

Turkey Vulture lunged at me, and before I knew it, he'd ripped my name tag from around my neck.

"The snatching of the name tag means you have not survived Survival Night! You are TAKEN."

That didn't sound good.

I raised my hand. "What do you mean *taken*?" I asked. "Taken where?"

Turkey Vulture smiled. "You'll find out when it happens, won't you?" he said, and handed my name tag back to me. I could see what he was thinking: that I'd be one of the first to go.

"The final surviving player delivers victory to her entire pack." Turkey Vulture locked eyes with each of us in turn. His were *wild*. "Now let Survival Night BEGIN!"

We all shot off in different directions up the sides of the volcano. I raced behind Cedar on the trail to our shelter, with Steve puffing heavily behind us. Once we were safely inside, we hunkered down and plotted our strategy.

"I think we should just stay here," I said. "We've got all the food and water we collected yesterday."

"Are you kidding?" Cedar said. "The Cold Bloods will come for us! I'm not going to sit around and *wait* for them to come steal our tags." She passed out a handful of berries. "Let's have a snack and move out."

"And *then* what?" I said.

"We do what Turkey Vulture told us to do," she said. "We move silently through the woods. And pounce!"

"Just let's stick together, okay?" I said.

I *still* didn't know my way around.

After we'd finished our berries, we snuck out of the shelter and made a run for the nearest line of trees. We hadn't gone ten feet before we felt rocks whizzing by our heads.

The Cold Bloods!

"Hey, you can't use ROCKS!" Cedar yelled at them. "That's against the rules!"

"Rules?" Newt scoffed. "There's no such thing as *rules* on Survival Night!"

"Run, little babies!" Scorpion called. "Run as fast as you can, because we're coming to get you!"

And we did.

CHAPTER 42

I was licking the last of the yellow rectangles when the balding ogre stepped into the cooking room.

"How'd you get that out, little guy?" he said, snatching my treat from the floor.

I whacked him, but his hand was so bandaged from the many wounds I had already inflicted upon him that he hardly noticed.

"Oh, don't worry, kitty," he said. "I bought a very *special* treat for you."

I did not trust this one bit, so I retreated to a safe position under the firebox.

"Here you go!" he said, throwing something at me.

It appeared to be a garish doll of some sort. The likeness was terrible, but I believe it was meant to be a mouse.

What did he think I was? A kitten? One of these idiot Earth cats? A . . . A . . .

What was that intoxicating smell?

It was coming from the purple mouse. I inched closer, and the smell grew stronger. It seemed to speak to me. *Come pounce! Come bite! Come shred me into pieces with your deadly back claws!*

It was as if my mind was not my own. Oh, the smell of this mouse doll! This beautiful purple mouse doll! What was inside of it? Happiness *itself*?

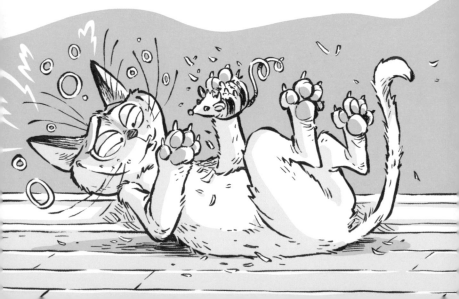

I ripped it to bits and rolled around in its stuffing.
This mouse was *the best thing* on this entire miserable
planet!

CHAPTER 43

Thursday Afternoon.

"Are you guys okay?" Cedar asked when we finally stopped running.

The Cold Bloods had been chasing us for what seemed like forever through the woods, but we lost them in the stinging nettles field. Cedar knew the safe path across, so we were able to make a clean getaway while Scorpion and the others got stuck there, howling in pain.

We regrouped at the base of the chain-link fence that blocked the path to the summit. They wouldn't ever think we'd go to a dead end on purpose.

At least, I *hoped* they wouldn't.

"I'm hungry," Steve said.

"I'm exhausted," I said. "I think we should stay here. Let the rest of the kids steal each other's tags."

"Come on, you guys—do you really want to give up so easily?" Cedar said.

Steve and I both shrugged. *I* was okay with it.

Then, out of the blue, Cedar started to cry.

"What's wrong?" I asked. Cedar was the *brave* one! The nature ninja! If she fell apart, what did that mean for the rest of us?

"I don't want to lose!" she said. "I'm sick of Scorpion and his stupid sidekicks. They're so mean!"

"Forget the Cold Bloods," I said. "After tomorrow, we'll never have to see them again."

"But we're all going to the same school!" she said. "There's only *one* middle school in this town."

My heart sank. The thought had never occurred to me. In Brooklyn, *no one* went to the same middle school. There were hundreds of them!

"I don't want them calling us forest failures in the hallway," Cedar said, kicking at a clump of moss. "I want to win the game!"

I remembered what Klawde had said to me this morning: *An army need not be stronger—only smarter. And crueler.*

I wasn't interested in cruelty. But the smart part I hoped we could manage.

"We aren't as big or as mean as the Cold Bloods," I said, "but we can hit them where it hurts."

"How?" Cedar asked.

"We steal their snacks."

Steve patted his belly. "I definitely like the sound of *that.*"

We made our plan: While the Cold Bloods were chasing the other teams, trying to steal their tags, we'd raid their shelter. They'd never expect it!

The only problem was that when we got to the

Cold Bloods' shelter, we discovered that it was empty. Abandoned.

"What do we do now?" Steve moaned.

"They've obviously built a new, secret lair, and we need to find it," Cedar said. "Steve, you go west. Rat and I will head east along the ridge."

It was late afternoon now, but between the cloudy skies and the dark forest, it seemed like nighttime.

We were creeping down a deer trail when we heard the snap of a twig.

Cedar immediately whirled around and ripped the tag from a kid who'd been trying to ambush us.

"Nice try, Otter!" she said. "I'm sure the rest of Swamp Team will miss you."

Otter didn't even have time to look disappointed before Turkey Vulture appeared out of nowhere and dragged him away, whimpering.

"Where is he *taking* him?" I whispered.

"I don't know," Cedar said. "And I don't want to find out. Come on! Let's keep moving."

I flinched at every forest sound I heard. I kept telling myself it was only a game. But it really didn't feel like one.

CHAPTER 44

I was no longer on vile Earth. I was rocketing through space, flying past exploding nebulas. I watched stars being born, and entire new galaxies bursting into being—all of them ready to bow down before me! I was not just the ruler of one planet. I ruled the entire universe! HA-HA-*HA*!

Then I woke from my nap.

I was still in the cooking room. The grinning father-Human stood amid the torn shreds of the purple mouse.

"Was that good, boy?" the father-Human said. "Do you want another?"

Did I? Of course I did!

I said, "Mrow!"

Oh *no*!

What had become of me? I had said it! The idiot Earth cat word!

These mouse dolls—this was how the Humans controlled felines. *This* was how they made Earth cats stupid! The **fiends**!

Another mouse doll landed at my feet, this one yellow and blue. Oh, the smell! The *smell*!

But I would not succumb to it. My will was titanium steel.

I stood up, scratched the father-Human on his hideous leg, and hurried downstairs. It was time to leave this planet of nightmares.

CHAPTER 45

Thursday Night.

"Are we there yet?" I whispered.

We'd been circling the top of Mount Eclipse for ages, trying and failing to find the Cold Bloods' new shelter.

"These guys are smarter than I thought," Cedar said.

It was raining now, and somewhere in the distance, coyotes had begun to howl.

My plan was a total failure.

Cedar wiped raindrops from her face. "It's okay, Rat. We're going to make it."

"It's getting dark! How are we going to find the shelter? How are we going to find Steve?"

"Hush!" she said.

"But—"

She held her finger to her lips. And that's when I heard it: the crack of a branch.

Something was creeping in our direction.

I don't want to get taken.

I don't want to get taken.

I don't want to get taken.

My heart banged in my chest like it would explode right out of me.

The cracking got louder, and then there was a huge **crash** as something enormous came rushing toward us in the darkness.

I screamed.

Then Cedar shouted, "STEVE!"

He was holding a woven basket full of leaves and food.

"Wild asparagus and salmonberries," Steve said. "The Cold Bloods' snacks!"

"Steve, you're a genius!" Cedar said as we stuffed berries into our mouths.

"Nobody's ever told me *that* before," Steve said, grinning.

Then we heard the sound of laughter.

Cruel laughter.

From somewhere came a voice.

"Did you *really* think we'd leave our shelter unguarded?"

I couldn't see him, but I knew it was Scorpion.

"You think we'd let you just waltz in and eat our snacks?" He cackled. "Fat chance, little babies!"

We heard Newt and Snake snickering. The sound seemed to come from everywhere and nowhere. Where were they? Were we surrounded? We crouched down behind a clump of ferns.

"We already wiped out the Fire Team," Snake called.

"And we finished off the Swamp Team!" Newt added.

"Are you three ready to be *taken*?" Scorpion yelled.

Cedar's eyes got fierce. "They're closing in on us,"

she whispered. "We've got to scatter, and then it's every man for himself. Only one of us needs to survive, remember?" She reached down to the mud of the path and spread it across her cheeks. *"Camouflage!"* she said. And then—like a shadow—she vanished.

"I guess it's just you and me, Rat," Steve said.

"That seems like a ba—"

All at once, the forest erupted.

Three shapes came hurtling at us. I hit the forest floor just as Newt went sailing over my head and crashed into a blackberry bush. A very *thorny* blackberry bush.

"Ow! Ow! Ow!" she yelped.

That must've hurt.

Snake and Steve grappled like a couple of professional wrestlers. But with a quick swipe of his right hand, Steve got his opponent's badge.

"Victory!" Steve yelled, holding Snake's tag high.

Then Scorpion appeared out of nowhere and snatched *Steve's* badge. Any second now, Turkey Vulture would appear and drag my pack mate away.

"Ha!" Scorpion yelled. "You're next, Rat! Prepare to be TAKEN!"

He came at me, but I dived forward through the brush. When I came out on the other side, the wet ground gave way, and I started sliding, headfirst, down the slope of Mount Eclipse.

CHAPTER 46

In the corner of the ogres' underground bunker, my teleporter awaited its ultimate mission: returning me to Lyttyrboks.

I inspected it one last time. Everything was in order. The green light on the fusion reactor blinked steadily. It was time to go.

But then—*hiss!*—I heard footsteps, and the long-furred ogre entered the bunker holding a box in her paws.

I glared at her.

She glared back.

"*Someone* needs to deal with these boxes if we're going to live in this place," the mother-Human said.

Up and down the stairs she kept coming and going, bringing down the boxes. She began to mark on them in that ugly scribble the Humans use to record their primitive language.

The task was endless, and I needed to leave! I would have to treat her as I did the father-ogre.

I walked up to her somewhat less hideous leg. Just as I was about to scratch her bloody, she turned to me.

"If you try it, I'll skin you alive and turn you into a fur hat."

Finally, a Human I could respect.

I stood down.

I had to wait until she went back upstairs—and stayed there. It took two naptimes, but at last she seemed to be gone for good. The hour was finally at hand!

CHAPTER 47

Thursday Night.

I don't know how long I rolled down the slope, or how long it took for my head to stop spinning once I reached the bottom.

I sat up. I was scratched all over but otherwise fine—except I had no idea where I was. I put on my deer ears. I couldn't hear anything.

What was I going to do now?

I stayed there for a while, thinking I was safe.

I should've known better.

"It's just you and us, Rat. We're the only ones left!" It was Newt, calling from somewhere up the hill. "Who would've thought you'd survive this long?"

"That girl pack mate of yours put up a good fight,

but she's with the others," Scorpion shouted. "Now it's *your* turn, rodent!"

Their voices were getting louder. They were closing in on me!

Without knowing which direction I was heading, I began to run.

Why *couldn't* I be rocketing across the universe with Klawde? This was the scariest night of my life!

"Oh, little *Raaaaaaat*," came Scorpion's voice. "We're right *behiiiiiind* you."

I ran faster. Where the path split, I went left, and pretty soon the trail widened. And then I wasn't in the forest anymore—I was in a clearing. Down below, I saw a dim yellow light.

It was coming from the porch of the Welcome Cabin.

Maybe I was saved after all!

With a giant burst of speed, I raced toward it. Scorpion's taunts began to fade behind me.

At the door, I paused. This was not only the Welcome Cabin—it was the home of the Forbidden Basket.

I could see my cell phone in it, right on top. It seemed to be calling to me.

I pushed open the window and climbed carefully inside. I grabbed the phone—it felt so good in my hands!—and pressed DAD.

"Raj?" he said.

"Hey, Dad," I said. "Look, it's against the rules for me to call, but I *really* want to say good night to Klawde. So can you find him, put the phone on speaker, and lay it down in front of him? And leave?"

"*Oooookay,*" he said. Dad clearly thought I was nuts, but he was going to do it anyway.

Which is why I didn't press MOM.

I heard the sound of him going down the stairs and placing the phone on the ground, and then the basement door shutting as he left.

"What is it?" said Klawde. He sounded impatient.

I was about to explain the whole situation, but the door of the Welcome Cabin started to open!

I talked as fast as I could. "If you REALLY are a great feline warrior, you need to come help me!" I said. "NOW!"

Then I hit the flashlight icon on my phone. The beam lit up the intruder, creeping toward me.

Turkey Vulture!

CHAPTER 48

I was **finally** entering the teleporter when the
father-Human returned.

Hiss!

He set his primitive communicator down in front of
me and retreated.

It was the boy-ogre calling. The battle had gone badly.

Little surprise. I certainly would not miss this Human's complaining while I was shaving the tails of my enemies!

I was about to hang up on him when something interesting happened.

There was shouting—I heard the word *help* many times—and the sound of a scuffle. The clash of combat.

Then the communicator went dead.

Had my Human fallen in battle? Had he been captured by his enemies?

Now *this* interested me.

Also, the boy-Human had begged me to mount a rescue operation, and let it never be said that the Lord High Emperor of All Cats shrinks from a challenge!

I would go save him.

There was only one way to get to him quickly: the family go-cart.

Thankfully, this vehicle operated on push-button technology. (Why couldn't the Humans do this with *everything*?) With a press of my paw, I started the engine; with another, I put it into drive mode and set the speed control.

The brake was out of the reach of my hind paws, but who needed brakes? What I needed was *speed*!

As for finding the boy-Human, that would be no problem. Because I had chipped him in his sleep, the tracker in my communicator showed me exactly where he was.

Even at the sluggish pace of—what was it now?—107 miles per hour, I began to purr as I rolled down the open road.

I was going off to battle again.

I felt **ALIVE**!

CHAPTER 49

Thursday Night.

Our counselor was totally, terrifyingly transformed.

His face and beard were covered in moss. His feet were muddy and bare, and in his dirty hand he carried a fat stick. Craziest of all, he now seemed to be wearing a bush. He was a forest nightmare come to life.

"**RAT!**" Turkey Vulture cried. "I knew the stench of civilization was strong on you, but I never expected *this*."

I was frozen in fear. My phone fell to the floor. "But the Cold Bloods were throwing rocks and—"

Turkey Vulture took another step toward me. "I don't care about *rocks*! Rocks are part of nature! But *you* have used what is unnatural!" he yelled. "Technology! How dare you ruin this beautiful game with such an outrage!"

He shook his stick at me. Was he going to hit me with it?

I certainly wasn't going to hang around to find out. I hopped up onto the desk, dived back out the window, and **ran**!

The rain had finally stopped, but the paths were all mud soup and I kept slipping and falling.

Up the slope of the volcano we raced, with Turkey

Vulture a stone's throw behind me—and closing in! How could he run so fast with all those branches and leaves on him?

There was only one direction to escape: **UP!**

Taking a running start, I scrambled up the trunk of a giant oak. I was climbing higher and higher when I heard Newt's high-pitched shriek.

"He's up there!" Newt yelled. "Trapped like the rat he is!"

She was right—I *was* trapped!

Even so, I climbed higher. I wasn't going to make it easy for them to take me. As I neared the tree's upper branches, I saw a flash of white light in the distance.

Was it lightning? Or—*please*—a rescue helicopter?

"Stand back!" Turkey Vulture shouted. He had reached the tree, and now *he* started climbing.

Scorpion's cruel laughter seemed to echo all around me. "Rat's about to get exterminated!" he yelled.

I gritted my teeth and kept going. I hoped the branches would hold me.

Suddenly, I saw movement in another tree, high up, near where I was! I squinted through the darkness. Something was making its way toward me, hopping from branch to branch, making a howling sound. Did they have *monkeys* in Oregon? Could wolves climb trees?

In another moment, it was in *my* tree—right above my head!

I knew it was the end. I was cornered: Turkey Vulture below me, and some kind of horrible tree-hopping forest beast above!

"I've almost got you, Rat!" Turkey Vulture called.

Then the creature from above came hurtling down.

I screamed and ducked, and it went flying past me.

Hissing as it went.

Klawde!

CHAPTER 50

I had never seen anything like it: My Human was being pursued up a tree by a monster. It appeared to be half-ogre and half-*plant*, and it obviously planned to devour my Human—or worse.

What a shame I couldn't bring THIS one through the teleporter!

But there was no time to lose if I wanted to save my Human. I quickly scaled the nearest tree and leaped branch to branch until I was directly above him and the squawking plant-beast.

I paused, took aim, and launched myself into the air.

Oh, the joy of gliding through the sky! The feel of the wind ruffling my fur! The glory of battle swelling my ferocious heart!

My aim was true, and I made a direct hit on the

plant-monster's head. My claws made quick work of its face.

My, but these earthlings injure easily!

"**AHHH!**" the monster screamed, and fell backward out of the tree.

Luckily for the plant-ogre, its leafy branches cushioned the impact of its fall. But they wouldn't protect it from the fury of my claws!

I jumped down and attacked at ground level. I showed the monster no mercy, but its strength was that of ten thousand cats. It grasped me by the neck and tore me off itself. Then it dangled me from its hideous leafy paw.

I yowled in fury and slashed at the beast, but my claws met nothing but air.

If this was to be my end, at least I had fought as no cat had ever fought before.

"A *CAT*!" the creature yelled. "Behold, campers, this vile and destructive creature! This killer of songbirds!

This murderer of chipmunks! This perfidious predator!"

I know—it *sounds* complimentary. But I took offense at the creature's tone.

The plant-monster stared me right in the eyes. "The rampage of you and your kind has gone on for far too long," it cried. "There will be no cats in the apocalypse— except for *dinner*. Now, who's hungry?"

"Hey, you can't do that!" my Human yelled down from above. "That's *my* cat!"

"I should have suspected! Well, he's NOT your cat anymore!" the plant-monster yelled. He shook me from head to tail. "Finders keepers, finders *eaters*!"

And that's when I spoke to him in his own barbaric tongue.

"Do your *worst*, plant-Human!" I cried.

The monster's hideous mouth fell open.

CHAPTER 51

Thursday Night.

I couldn't believe it! Klawde had come to *save* me! How did he even find me?

From high above, I watched as he attacked Turkey Vulture. But then the counselor managed to grab him and hold Klawde out of striking distance. And now he was threatening to *eat* him!

I had to swallow my fear. And it was then that I found my inner battle cat.

"You can do whatever you want to **me**, you crazy lunatic!" I cried. "But not to my **CAT**!"

I flung myself out of the tree. I had no plan, other than to land on Turkey Vulture.

Which I did.

It *hurt*. Both of us.

Turkey Vulture lost his grip on Klawde, who jumped out of the way.

"Run, Klawde," I called. "Run! *Run!*"

Klawde hesitated—I could tell he didn't want to leave me. **"Go!"** I cried.

And he did.

I turned to the Cold Bloods, expecting a fight. But they weren't paying any attention to me. Instead, they turned to Turkey Vulture, who was lying on the ground in a daze.

"Were you being serious about eating Rat's cat?" Scorpion asked. "Because that's *messed up*."

Newt nodded. "Yeah, it's *totally* psycho."

"You heard it talk, didn't you?" Turkey Vulture cried. "That animal *spoke* to me!"

"You mean," Scorpion said, "when it meowed?"

Turkey Vulture's eyes were wild. "No, no! It spoke in

English. Don't you understand? Cats are **evolving**!"

Scorpion looked at Newt, then at me. "Game over, you guys. Turkey Vulture's lost the plot. Let's go to the tent."

They took off their name tags and dumped them on the ground.

"*Tent?*" I said. "What tent?"

"The tent where everyone else is," Scorpion said. "What did you *think* happened when someone got taken?"

I didn't really want to say.

Off in the distance, I saw the flash of white light again. Then came the red glow of taillights and a song, fading into the night.

We're not gonna take it!

NO! We ain't gonna take it!

CHAPTER 52

Oh, what a joy it was to watch my Human attack his enemy! He sailed through the air like a true feline commando.

Although I did not like his prospects against the plant-ogre, his brave actions had given me the chance to retreat.

Sometimes a great leader must know when to leave his troops behind. As the saying goes, *There are always more soldiers, but there is only one warlord.*

I would miss the young ogre after all, I thought as I entered the motorized go-cart. Back at the controls, I finally discovered the button for flight mode.

Except I did not. Instead of levitating, the car filled with the dreadful noise Humans call music.

We're not gonna take it ANYMOOOOORE!

Hmm. It *was* sort of catchy.

CHAPTER 53

Thursday Night.

There they were—the Swamp Team, the Fire Team, Snake, Steve, and Cedar—eating hot dogs and s'mores inside a big, cozy tent.

Cedar came running up to me. "Rat, you're the only one with a name tag! You *won*!"

"A Banerjee always finishes what she starts!" I said.

"What *she* starts?" Steve asked.

"I said *he*!" I said. "What *he* starts."

"Rat didn't win," Scorpion said. "We just stopped playing!"

"So what?" Cedar said. "If you guys quit, *we* win. Right, Turkey Vulture?"

But Turkey Vulture didn't seem to hear her. He was

still babbling about talking cats and how they were going to take over the world.

"I tell you all," he whispered, "the apocalypse is nearer than we *think*!"

We stayed up almost the whole night and—believe it or not—I was actually sad when the time came to leave.

As we were walking out through the Camp Eclipse arch, Steve leaned in to me. "So, what you said about your cat," he whispered. "That was all *true*?"

"Let's just say what happens at Camp Apocalypse *stays* at Camp Apocalypse," I said.

"Except us being friends," Cedar said. "Right?"

I couldn't help smiling. "Yeah, except that."

"You guys *are* losers," Scorpion said, passing by us.

But we didn't care.

We got to the parking lot, where our parents were waiting.

"You guys have to start calling me Wolf now," Steve said. "What's your real name?"

"Uh, Raj," I said.

"*Raj?* Your name is *Raj?*" Steve said. "Real creative forest name, Rat."

"How about you?" I said, turning to Cedar. "What's your real name?"

"Wouldn't *you* like to know!" Cedar said, and then darted into her parents' car.

"So, you made it through nature camp!" Mom said when I got into the Prius. "That wasn't so bad, was it?"

I shrugged. "No, I guess not."

I felt pretty good about things. But as we turned down our street, I saw the telephone poles with the LOST CAT posters on them, a picture of Chad looking back at me. And I didn't feel so good anymore.

Because pretty soon, my cat would be gone, too.

CHAPTER 54

I took a nap, lapped up some white liquid, and read the *Wall Street Journal* on the toilet one last time. I was ready to leave—*again*—when the most unexpected thing of all happened.

I heard the voice of my boy-Human.

How in the eighty-seven moons had he survived? Did he manage to murder all three of his enemies? *Alone?*

I was so proud!

I took my paw off the teleport button. Even an Evil Warlord must say goodbye to a soldier who fought so valiantly!

The boy-Human found me in the basement. He was dirty and scratched, like a true warrior.

"I wish you didn't have to go," he said. "But I understand that *your* fight is back home."

"I am sorry you will not be coming to Lyttyrboks to share in my glorious victory," I said. "But you will do well here on Earth. Perhaps one day you will even rule it! You will be the Kind Earthling Warlord Human."

The boy-ogre bared his teeth at me with his lips curled up, in the hideous grimace the Humans call a smile.

Why did they *do* that?

As for me, I paid the boy-Human the ultimate sign of respect: the Twining Curl. I rubbed against him, allowing my tail to wind, briefly and gently, around his shin.

And with that, I entered the teleporter, pressed the button, and said goodbye to this dismal planet known as Earth.

Good riddance!

CHAPTER 55

Friday Afternoon.

I stayed down in the basement until I heard my parents get home from Mom's tennis match.

"Here, kitty kitty kitty!" I heard Dad calling.

He's not here, I thought sadly. *He'll never be here again.*

"Have you seen Klawde?" Dad asked when I came upstairs.

"Is something wrong?" Mom asked when she saw my face.

I told them the lie that I'd prepared—that while they were gone, the family who had lived in the house before us came looking for their lost cat:

Klawde.

"Some cats attach to places more than people, so that's why he came back here after they moved," I said. "At least, that's what they told me."

"Oh, *Raj*," Mom said, and gave me a hug.

"I sure did love that little guy," Dad said, and wiped a tear from his eye with one of his bandaged fingers.

Yeah, me too.

I went to my room, got into bed, pulled the covers up to my chin, and fell asleep.

It was the green flash that woke me.

I sat up immediately.

"That was *not* lightning," I heard my mom saying. "It's sunny out! We need to have an electrician look at the wiring in this old house."

I shot out of bed and raced down the stairs, and that's when I heard it—a faint "MROW!"

It was coming from the basement!

I ran downstairs three steps at a time.

"MROW?"

The teleporter shook, the door opened, and out stepped . . .

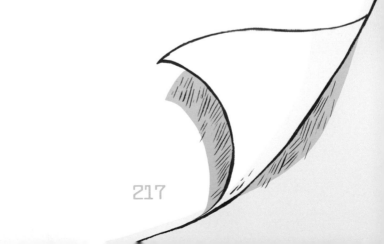

Chad.

I sank down to the floor.

Chad waddled toward me, meowing loudly. There was a note attached to his collar.

EPILOGUE

It felt almost like old times. Mom was reading, Dad was watching TV, and I was just sitting there, bored. But at least tonight I was waiting for Cedar and Wolf to come over.

In the two weeks since Camp Apocalypse had ended, I'd spent a lot of time hanging out with them. They showed me around Elba, which turned out to be a pretty cool place. My parents would barely let me leave my block back in Brooklyn, but here I could bike wherever I wanted. There were two ice-cream shops, a nickel arcade, and even a good comic book store—all within biking distance.

The only thing I wanted now was to get my cat back.

Mom and Dad kept telling me I could have a new one. But how could any other cat compare to Klawde?

Then, out of nowhere, it happened *again*: a bright flash of green light.

I jumped up from the chair and went running to the front door. And right when I got there:

DING-DONG!

I flung open the door.

It was **Klawde**!

I picked him up and began kissing him all over his furry little face.

Klawde hissed. "Put me down, you *disgusting* ogre!" he thundered. "Don't you understand what has happened?!"

"You missed me so much you came back for a visit?"

"Don't be absurd," Klawde said.

He told me that he had overthrown General Ffangg and reconquered Lyttyrboks with lightning speed—only to have been betrayed. AGAIN.

"And this time by the *last* cat I would ever have suspected!" Klawde said. "**Flooffee-Fyr!** Who could've imagined that simpering lackey would have the guts to betray me? I respect him now, yes! But he shall taste my **REVENGE**!"

"I'm just glad to have my kitty back," I said.

"Don't *ever* call me that again, or I will vaporize you across ten galactic quadrants!" Klawde said.

He swatted me, leaving a bloody scratch on my finger. It hurt a little, but I didn't care.

My evil alien warlord cat was home.

ABOUT THE AUTHORS

Although a worthless Human, **Johnny Marciano** has redeemed himself somewhat by chronicling the glorious adventures of Klawde, Evil Alien Warlord Cat. His lesser work concerns the pointless doings of other worthless Humans, in books such as *The Witches of Benevento*, *The No-Good Nine*, and *Madeline at the White House*. He currently resides on the planet New Jersey.

Emily Chenoweth is a despicable Human living in Portland, Oregon, where the foul liquid known as rain falls approximately 140 days a year. Under the top secret alias Emily Raymond, she has collaborated with James Patterson on numerous best-selling books. There are three other useless Humans in her family, and two extremely ignorant Earth cats.